THE SPIRIT OF THE

THE CASE OF THE HAUNTED GHOST

LIZ HEDGECOCK

combination of a huge library and a giant room full of people, though none of it could be trusted. Waste of time, if you ask me.

'You won't need the internet,' said the inspector. 'This is for data entry. I want you to set up a spreadsheet and log the files you read. Nothing elaborate: just file date, officer in charge, date and nature of crime, resolved or not. You'll be able to whip through stacks of paperwork.'

'Oh,' said Steph. She looked as disappointed as I felt. 'I thought—'

'You thought you'd be chasing criminals through the afterlife?' Inspector Farnsworth gave her a smile which I think was meant to be kind. It looked indulgent to me. 'What happened in October was… I'm not sure what it was, but that sort of thing happens perhaps once every ten years.'

'Ten years?' cried Steph. 'Surely you don't expect me to spend ten years working through every file in this room, sir?' She waved a hand at the rows of tall filing cabinets that lined the room. I saw her point. Apart from anything else, imagine the dust.

'Not at all, Constable,' said the inspector. 'But in order to get permission for you to be at the Bridewell, and have a chance of investigating with your colleague here' – he beamed at me, and I remembered why I liked him again – 'I need to show that you aren't just sitting in a largely-disused police station with a stack of magazines and a bacon butty.'

'It didn't bother anyone when the rest of the team did that,' muttered Steph.

Inspector Farnsworth's eyebrows drew together, which, as far as I could tell, signified maximum crossness. 'The rest of the team, Constable Sharpe, didn't have access to the resources that you do.' He gave me a little nod. 'If you're reading through the files, there's every chance something may jog Nora's memory. Then . . . another cold case?'

Steph closed her mouth in a way that gave her a particularly grumpy expression. 'I suppose so. Go on then.'

The inspector raised his eyebrows. 'I wasn't actually giving you a choice, Constable Sharpe. Now, I think you can enter, let's say seventy-five files a day when you're here. I'll expect a one-page headline report every Friday. Numbers and offending patterns, no more. If nothing else, it could be a valuable record for policing history. Yes.' He looked thoughtful, then wandered out of the room as if he'd forgotten what he came in for.

I returned to the present day, and the present file. 'So what's the offence this time?' I asked brightly.

'Drunkenness. Again.' Steph typed rapidly on the laptop, then closed the file and tossed it on the pile to her right. 'Nora, how drunk did someone have to be to get arrested around here?'

'Depends,' I said. 'Mostly on who was on duty. There were a couple of religious types who, if they even saw someone a bit unsteady on their feet near a pub, they'd have them. Or if card players were on shift, they'd fill the cells as quickly as possible so that they could get on with a game.'

Steph frowned. 'That's awful. What if someone ended up with a criminal record and they weren't drunk? That could ruin their life.'

'Oh, if they knew the family they put a false name. It wasn't as if anyone was checking.'

Steph cast a look of pure evil at the stack of files. 'So I'm spending my time logging cases which are probably lies from start to finish.'

'I wouldn't say that,' I said, regretting my honesty. 'Some of the arrests were of beggars and vagrants with nowhere to go on the coldest nights of the year. If nothing else, they'd be out of the bad weather with a bowl of soup and a hunk of bread.'

'That's something,' said Steph, but she still seemed troubled. How I wished I had kept mum about the somewhat elastic nature of justice at the Bridewell.

'I'm sure you'll find a really interesting case soon,' I said, hoping with all my heart that she would. If Steph decided she'd had enough and returned to her colleagues at Erskine Street, I would be alone again. Well, not alone, exactly. There would be an officer upstairs during the station's hours of operation, reading a book or dozing while they waited for concerned members of the public who never came. And there would be Superintendent Hicks, another former employee, who had unbent sufficiently to speak to me occasionally in the course of his unvarying rounds of the Bridewell. But it would never be the same.

'How many files have you done today?' I asked, keeping my tone light and pleasant.

'Forty.'

'Already? But it's only quarter past nine. Maybe you should take a break.'

'I'll take a break when I get to seventy-five,' said Steph, grimly. 'I want to get a hundred and fifty done by lunch. The sooner I get through these files and back to proper police work, the better I'll like it. This is worse than Sergeant Doughty's required reading.' She sighed. 'You may as well carry on with your magazine. I'll let you know if anything interesting comes up.' Her tone suggested she thought that extremely unlikely.

'Thank you,' I said, and returned to Nigel Slater. This week he was talking about something called tenderstem broccoli. It looked thin and weedy to me.

All of a sudden there was a rattle from upstairs, followed by a creak. 'Bit early for Superintendent Hicks,' said Steph.

'That's not him. Apart from anything else, he can't

make floorboards creak.'

'Good point,' said Steph. 'It might actually be a member of the public. I'd better go and meet them.'

'I don't think you need to do that,' I said, as we heard a splintering sound, followed by low, irritated muttering. 'They're coming down.' And I was right, for two minutes later, there was a knock at the file-room door and in walked Inspector Farnsworth. He had been neat and professional the last time I had seen him, but now he was breathless, with the top button of his shirt undone and his tie slightly askew.

'Sorry to intrude,' he said, 'but I've received word of a case. One where your particular talents' – and he looked at me – 'will be most useful.'

Oh, I could have hugged the man. A case! An opportunity to put my not-inconsiderable detective skills into practice! And a chance to leave the station! I glanced at Steph, who wore the alert expression of a gun dog. 'Tell me more.'

CHAPTER 2

'So what's the case?' asked Steph.

I crossed my fingers under the table. A kidnapping, perhaps? Or a robbery? Or even – murder? Ooh yes, a nice juicy murder. Imagine the headline: *GHOST COP SOLVES CASE*.

'The Chief didn't give me much detail,' said Inspector Farnsworth. He pulled out a chair and sat down. 'What I do know is that it's at the Athenaeum. He's a member, you see.'

'The Athenaeum?' said Steph. 'What's that?'

'It's a private club in Liverpool city centre,' I said. 'For gentlemen to engage in conversation and read the papers. That sort of thing.'

'Women can be members too, Nora,' said Inspector Farnsworth. 'But yes, that's what it is. The Chief says there have been mysterious disturbances.'

Mentally, I waved goodbye to the front page of the *Daily Post*, or whatever the paper of the day was. 'Of a supernatural kind?'

'He said "things that go bump in the night". Except they've been doing it in the day. And doing more than just bump. As for detail, we'll have to find out when we get there.'

'So I'm coming to the Athenaeum?'

'Well, yes.'

I leapt up and clapped my hands. 'I've always wanted to see inside! All those men in expensive suits going in and coming out.'

'Nora, you're in the table again,' said Steph.

'Sorry.' I backed out. 'You ought to be used to it by now. It's not as if I can feel anything. Anyway, it's not important. Let's go to the Athenaeum!' I turned to the inspector. 'Are we taking a car?'

Ten minutes later, we were driving through the middle of Liverpool. I stared around me at the buildings and the people. I would have found it less surprising if everything had been strange to me, but every so often I recognised a building, or a face that reminded me of someone I had known. But the building would be sandwiched by two I had never seen before, and the face would be on top of an outfit no one would have dared to wear in public in my day, or with a ridiculous haircut. I felt as if I was lurching between past and present.

'Here we are,' said the inspector, parking by the Old Post Office pub. Now that was a place I knew, though of course I had never entered it. 'We can walk from here.'

'Why are people wandering in and out?' I said, as we passed the Bluecoat, watching someone hold up one of those fancy calculator things that Steph persisted in calling a phone. 'Won't they disrupt the architects? Or are they artists?'

'It's an arts centre nowadays, Nora,' said Steph. 'Anyone can go in.'

'Oh.' She got out of the car and opened my door, though in truth I could just as easily have gone through it.

'It's a hop, skip, and a jump away,' said Inspector Farnsworth.

'I know,' I said. I walked along a narrow street with multicoloured umbrellas hanging above it. Sometimes I found the modern world very confusing. Why put a whole lot of perfectly good umbrellas in the air? Now if they'd been available to borrow, that would have made sense. I looked over my shoulder. 'Come on, then.'

Both Inspector Farnsworth and Steph had stopped. 'Nora, it's here,' said the inspector.

'It isn't.' I pointed down the street. 'It's this way, opposite the church.'

'It's definitely here, Nora,' called Steph. 'It says: *The Athenaeum.*'

'But it's this way.' I kept walking until I was at the

end of the street, then scanned the scene. There was Church Street, busy as usual, but with the busyness of a different century.

And there the Athenaeum . . . wasn't. In its place was a different building. And the church was gone too. I looked again to make sure, then gasped as someone walked through me from behind. 'Aargh!' I moaned, and sank to my knees.

'Nora!' Steph ran towards me. 'What is it? Are you all right?'

'I don't know.' I closed my eyes to shut out the unfamiliarity.

'Is it not what you expected?' Her voice was softer than usual. That, strangely, made me pull myself together. I'd lived through the Great War, for heaven's sake. Time went on, and things changed. I had to get used to that if I was going to have any sort of life in this modern world. 'I'm fine,' I said, and got to my feet.

'I'd offer you an arm if I could,' said Steph.

'I'd take it if I could,' I replied, and followed her to where Inspector Farnsworth was waiting.

'I imagine they've moved buildings,' he said.

'So I won't get to see the Athenaeum I would have known,' I said. 'Never mind. I'm sure this will be just as impressive.'

'I'm sure it will,' said the inspector, and rang the bell.

***

'It's hard to explain,' said our guide, a tall, slim, smartly dressed young man who had introduced himself as Jude, the concierge. I'd thought that concierges only worked in posh hotels, but looking around me, I could entirely understand why he was there.

The entrance hall was beautiful. I gazed at the furniture and paintings, then met Steph's glare and tuned back in to what Jude was saying, with reluctance.

'I feel rather embarrassed to have brought you two here,' he said, and indeed his cheeks had flushed a delicate shade of pink. 'It's not as if I can point to anything specific, even. But some of our members have complained of – a frisson.'

'A frisson?' said Inspector Farnsworth, looking dubious.

'I know,' said Jude. 'It's usually in the newsroom, but occasionally it's in the reading room. And a researcher with a pass to the stacks almost fainted. We had to revive her with a strong cup of coffee and a Danish pastry.'

'Can you describe this frisson?' asked Steph.

'I haven't felt it myself,' said Jude. 'But people have used phrases such as "someone walking over my grave", "a shiver down my spine", or "a feeling of impending doom".'

'Gosh,' said Inspector Farnsworth.

'It probably sounds like nothing, but we don't want our members to be uncomfortable.' Jude smiled. 'So we're very glad that Dickie Strachan said he would get his best officers on the case. I had no idea that the force employed, er, specialists in these matters. I really am grateful to you.'

I leaned towards Steph. 'Ask him if anything physical has happened,' I whispered. 'Things moving or breaking, for instance.' I don't know why I bothered to whisper; Jude's gaze slipped over me as if I wasn't there. It's most discomfiting when a handsome young man completely ignores you. Even if they can't help it.

'Have there been any physical disturbances?' asked Steph.

Jude considered this. He looked more handsome when he was slightly perplexed. 'Nothing's been broken, certainly. I would definitely have remembered, because it would have been reported. The only thing I can think of is that sometimes when I enter the newsroom to check it prior to opening, the periodicals have been disarranged. A newspaper on the floor, or open on the table. I just assumed it was missed when we locked up. So I put things right and thought nothing of it.'

'How long has this been going on?' asked the inspector.

'The first complaint came in about ten days ago,' said Jude. 'As I said, I'm sorry to have dragged you both out on what must seem a trivial matter.'

'Can we see the newsroom, please?' asked Steph.

'Yes, of course,' said Jude. 'If you don't mind, I'll act as if I'm showing you round as prospective members. The room is likely to be in use, and I don't wish to alarm anyone.'

I urged myself to be strong as we climbed the spiral staircase. I felt as if I was short of breath, though that couldn't be the case. 'Are you OK?' whispered Steph.

'I think so.' That was as definite as I could be.

'Here we are,' said Jude, and opened the door to a luxurious room with red velvet seats which matched the monogrammed carpet and the heavy curtains. It was lined with bookshelves, drawers, and cabinets. I could have spent many happy hours there when I was alive, and I cursed the Spanish flu that had taken away the opportunity. 'I'll let you walk around and get a feel for things.'

We split up and slowly patrolled the room. I kept to the edge, careful not to disturb the few people who were deep in newspapers or magazines. Lucky things. I would have loved to sneak up and read over their shoulders, but I didn't want to be mistaken for the mysterious frisson that was plaguing the club.

I gazed at the gilt-lettered drawer fronts, the bound

sets of *Punch*, the view from the large windows, and felt nothing. I sidled up to Steph, who was surveying the room. 'Anything?'

She shook her head. 'What a beautiful room,' she said, presumably for Jude's benefit.

'Could we see the reading room?' Inspector Farnsworth asked.

'Of course,' said Jude, and led us up another flight of stairs.

This room was, if anything, even more beautiful, dark green instead of red, with large paintings on the wall in pastel shades. I was sure they signified something, but I had no idea what. And I didn't have time to think about it, because a wave of nausea washed over me. I hurried to a vacant chair, hoping it would pass.

Steph came and sat next to me. 'Can you feel it too?' she whispered.

I nodded, and put my head between my knees. 'Feel sick,' I murmured. 'Do you?'

Steph shook her head. 'A bit chilly and twitchy, that's all. Can you see anything?'

I willed myself to my feet and walked around, keeping well clear of the readers and screwing up my eyes against the pale, penetrating winter light that streamed into the room. Was that a—? No, just a curtain moving slightly in the breeze. Or was it?

I continued to scan the room. The lower half of the

curtain was slightly blurred, as if the air had grown thicker and become a haze, but that was all I could see. And when I looked away and back, it had gone.

'Something's here,' I said. 'But whatever it is, it won't show itself. Maybe if we wait a few minutes…'

We sat in a silence punctuated only by Jude asking in a whisper whether we could feel the frisson, or whether we would like refreshments. Eventually, I shook my head. 'I don't think we'll get any further.' Even the nausea had passed. 'It's gone.'

'I don't think we'll have any luck today,' said Inspector Farnsworth.

Steph gave Jude her card. 'If anything else happens, please give me a ring or leave a message and we'll come back.'

'Thank you so much for your time,' said Jude. 'Are you sure you wouldn't like a cup of tea or coffee?'

'I'd love to,' said the inspector, 'but we ought to be getting on.'

'I quite understand,' said Jude, and took us downstairs.

None of us spoke until we were in the car. 'I felt something,' said Inspector Farnsworth.

'So did I,' said Steph. 'And Nora definitely did. I wonder why it wouldn't show itself to her?' She turned in her seat. 'Any ideas, Nora?'

'Search me,' I said, and grinned, but my emotions threatened to bubble over. Why wouldn't whatever was there show itself? Why had I felt so ill? And what if the others thought I was useless and didn't let me leave the station again? I had had a taste of freedom and craved more, but I cursed the spirit who had seemed determined to thwart me today.

CHAPTER 3

Back at the Bridewell, Steph returned to the file room, opened her laptop and reached for the next folder. I was in no mood to settle, though. I stared at a recipe for pan-fried chicken with cream and almonds, but I wasn't keen. In my mind, almonds are for cakes, or sugared, in paper bags from the sweet shop.

Steph looked up from her file. 'Do you want to talk about it?'

'About what?'

'Nora, you clearly have something on your mind. You're twitching.'

'Yes, I am. I'm annoyed that I'm stuck here.'

Steph shrugged. 'So am I. Welcome to the police.' She glanced at the file and began typing on the laptop. *Tippy-tappy-tippy-tappy.* It was enough to drive someone mad. Then again, in my day it had been the scratchy-scratchy of a metal nib or a lead pencil, or the thumpy-thumpy of the typewriters in the clerks' room.

'Shall I put the radio on?' said Steph.

'Thanks for asking, but no. It'll either be classical music or that noise you call patio.'

'Do you mean garage?'

'Probably.'

'OK. Whatever.' She returned to her typing and I read a paragraph about rare-breed hens.

'Maybe something else will happen at the Athenaeum and that nice concierge will invite us back,' I said.

'Maybe.'

'He was ever so handsome.'

Steph shrugged. 'Didn't really notice.'

I goggled at her. 'You didn't notice? Aren't police officers meant to be observant any more?'

Steph laughed. 'If he was a suspect, it would be different.'

I shook my head in disappointment. As far as I could tell, Steph thought of nothing besides work. Honestly, sometimes she seemed more of a machine than a young woman like me. Not that I can think of myself as young now, I suppose. But when you've spent a hundred years or thereabouts stuck in your twenties, you get to know yourself pretty well. Then I recalled that, unlike me, Steph had a life outside the station. *You don't know what she does once she leaves the Bridewell at night,* I thought. *Maybe she goes out dancing, or to the flicks. Maybe she has a beau, but she doesn't like to talk about him.*

'Do you have a boyfriend?' The words were out before I knew it.

Slowly, Steph raised her head. 'No, I don't. And I'd appreciate it if you don't ask personal questions when I'm trying to work.'

'Sorry I spoke.' I folded my arms and glared at a picture of mushrooms, which were apparently foraged.

For some time, the only noise was the rustle of pages, the tip-tap of the laptop, and an occasional light thud as another file was put on the pile. I considered asking Steph to turn the page for me – I was sick of chicken recipes – but I couldn't bring myself to do it.

I heard a knock and my heart leapt. Could it be Inspector Farnsworth with another case? Or even a member of the public with something for us to investigate? Then I glanced at the clock and my heart slumped in my chest. I knew exactly who it would be.

Steph was already out of her chair. 'I'll get that.' Off she went, humming a little tune.

The door opened, followed by chatter that was too low to hear. I got up and walked a little way down the corridor. 'I'll just finish the entry I'm on,' said Steph, 'then I'm ready.'

The other person sighed. 'All right. But I'm

coming with you to make sure you don't start another one. I know what you're like.'

I rushed back to my seat and presently two sets of footsteps came downstairs. 'Mind that step, Tasha,' said Steph.

'Good grief,' said Tasha. 'This place is a deathtrap. Why don't you work upstairs in one of the offices?'

'It's easier to be where the files are,' said Steph.

I tried not to scowl as they came in. Steph sat down at the laptop, and Tasha— I gasped as she pulled out my chair, with me still in it. 'Steph!' I cried.

Steph frowned at me and flapped her hand in a *move, then* gesture.

'Is something wrong with this chair?' Tasha asked, flicking back her shiny auburn plait. Somehow, she managed to make the police uniform look elegant.

'No, it's fine,' said Steph, completely ignoring me. 'Just a moth.'

I jumped up as Tasha was about to sit, stormed through the table and loomed over Steph, hands on hips. 'I am *not* a moth, thank you very much. When will you tell her about me? I mean, she should be able to see me. I'm not hiding.'

'Won't be a minute, Tasha,' said Steph. 'Two more fields to populate.'

'I'm still here.' I jumped up and down and waved my arms in front of the laptop screen. 'Talk to me.'

'Pesky moth,' muttered Steph, waving me away.

22

'What am I, a dirty secret?' I yelled in her ear.

'Where do you want to go for lunch?' asked Tasha. 'I need to be at my desk in forty minutes or Doughty will come after me. You know what he's like when Huw's out of the office. The Great Dictator.'

'Done,' said Steph. She pressed a couple of keys, closed the laptop and put another file on the pile. 'Let's see what takes our fancy.'

'You're on,' said Tasha, and beamed at her. 'All work and no play makes Steph a dull girl.'

'Less of the dull,' said Steph. 'And it's woman, if you don't mind.'

The pair of them left, chatting, and I was alone with my thoughts. They weren't pleasant company.

I deserve a break too, I thought. But as I couldn't leave the station unless I was on official business, my options were limited. After some thought, I wandered upstairs and out to the yard. Perhaps chatting to a police horse would make me feel better.

My favourite, a fine chestnut who was only slightly transparent, was standing in the middle of the yard, snorting gently and scraping a hoof on the cobbles. 'All right there, Prince?' I asked, stroking his nose. I had no idea what his name was, but he was a very regal horse.

'Nice day for it,' said a voice behind me, and I jumped.

'Don't do that!' I snapped, wheeling round. 'You'll

frighten Prince.'

'Don't speak to me like that, Nora Norris,' Superintendent Hicks snapped back. 'In fact, as a matron, you probably shouldn't address me at all.'

'Tough,' I replied. 'And I'm a constable, not a matron.'

He harrumphed, sounding rather like Prince. 'Only by the grace of that Inspector Farnsworth. A sorry excuse for an inspector he is, too. Looks as if he slept in his clothes. Absolute disgrace.' He pulled down the points of his waistcoat and smoothed his grey hair. 'What happened to spit and polish, eh?' He took a pipe from his jacket pocket and began to fill it. 'Anyway, where were you two this morning? The file room was empty when I did my rounds. I hope you weren't shirking your duties.'

Cheek. I drew myself up to my full height, not that it was particularly impressive, and stuck my chin in the air. 'I was out on a case with Steph, if you must know.'

'Were all the men busy?'

'We're as good as men any day, if not better. They needed my particular expertise.'

He squished the tobacco into his pipe and took out a box of matches. 'Who did?'

'The Athenaeum, in town. It's a private members' club.'

'Oh, the Athenaeum.' He struck a match on the

wall and lit his pipe. The tobacco glowed white, and pale smoke drifted upwards. At least ghost pipes didn't stink like real ones. He puffed for a few seconds to get it going. 'Nice place, that.'

Something in the superintendent's tone told me he wasn't trying to put one over on me, for once. 'Were you a member?' I asked.

'Thought about it,' he replied. He took a long draw on the pipe and blew a smoke ring. 'Went a few times with a friend, but it was too expensive for me, with a young family and all. Besides, John could always get me a guest pass.'

For a moment I was struck dumb with resentment. What a world it was for men, where they took the best jobs and their friends got them into smart places, while girls like me ended up doing the dirty work for a pittance and sharing a bedroom with their sisters. But I swallowed the bitterness back down. 'The old club, or the new one? I only remember the old one.'

'Mostly the new one,' said Superintendent Hicks, 'if by that you mean the one by the Bluecoat. Anyway, what's been going on there?'

'Ghost causing bother,' I said. 'Hid from us, though.'

'Don't blame him,' said the superintendent. 'He probably took one look at you and decided he was better off elsewhere. That's a thought, Nora, you could hire yourself out as an exorcist. Scaring ghosts away, ha!' And with that parting shot he stomped off, chuckling to himself.

I stamped my foot, knowing he wouldn't hear me, and rested my cheek against Prince's shoulder. *I hate him*, I muttered. But even as rage coursed through my veins, my brain was churning. Superintendent Hicks had visited the Athenaeum several times, and while he wasn't a member, he was as good as. Perhaps the ghost *was* like him, and had hidden from me because he had decided I wasn't fit to be in his company. I felt the sensation of tears welling up, but of course there was nothing.

Will you let hurt feelings and bruised pride get in the way of seeing that justice is done, Nora? I asked myself, sternly. *No, you will not. You will do your duty.* And as Prince let out a whinny of agreement, I resolved to speak to Steph as soon as she returned from whichever sandwich shop or takeaway she had visited this time. I had a feeling my news would be much more exciting than whatever she and that Tasha had found to talk about.

CHAPTER 4

Superintendent Hicks stood by the police car, arms folded. 'I'll go if I can sit in the front.'

'You do realise that will seem weird,' said Steph. 'One police officer in the front and one in the back.'

'Those are my terms.'

Inspector Farnsworth looked at Steph enquiringly and she sighed. 'Fine, whatever. Just get in, if you don't mind.'

'You mean "Would you be so kind as to enter the vehicle, Superintendent?"'

Steph turned to the inspector. 'He's being difficult. I don't think this will work.'

'Oh, all right,' said Superintendent Hicks, and slid into the vehicle.

Steph grimaced. 'Just because you can, it doesn't mean you should.'

'And you thought I was trouble,' I murmured.

Superintendent Hicks poked his head through the

window. 'I heard that, Nora.'

Our second trip to the Athenaeum, the day after our first, promised to be an interesting affair. For one thing, Superintendent Hicks was still refusing to show himself to Inspector Farnsworth, so the inspector had to trust to Steph and me. For a moment, I thought what a fine piece of mischief it would be to invent a police officer only I could see, but I suspected I would slip up. Besides, as I had been little use in the previous expedition, I didn't plan on doing anything that might mean my exclusion.

So I got into the back of the car without complaint. At least this time I could enjoy the ride, knowing that the main burden of the investigation was lifted from me.

'I phoned ahead,' said Inspector Farnsworth, as we parked by the pub again. 'How do we handle things?'

'When you say things,' said Superintendent Hicks, who had spent the journey staring out of the windows and watching the inspector drive, 'I hope you don't mean me and Nora.'

'Not at all,' said Steph. 'However, now that you mention it, I think I should partner you and Inspector Farnsworth should partner Nora.'

The superintendent drew himself up. 'You can't partner me: you're a constable. Remember your place, please.'

'I may be a constable, but I can see and hear you

and the inspector can't,' countered Steph. 'Unless you do something about that, the arrangement stands.'

Inspector Farnsworth turned in his seat. 'I have no idea what the superintendent said, but is he always like this?'

'Yes,' Steph and I said, together.

'I could refuse to work with all of you,' said Superintendent Hicks.

'In that case, you'll have to stay in the car,' said Steph, getting out. 'Nora can only leave the station on official assignments, and I assume it's the same for you.' She opened the front passenger door. 'Coming, or not?'

A minute or two later, we were in the entrance hall of the Athenaeum and I had another chance to admire Jude. 'See, he *is* handsome,' I murmured to Steph, but she ignored me.

'Now we have more idea what we're dealing with, Jude, I've brought a piece of specialist kit.' She pulled out a small black box with red buttons and a tiny screen. 'This will help us detect paranormal activity.'

Jude nodded sagely. 'Oh yes, that should help a lot.'

Superintendent Hicks walked over. 'Has she really got a ghost detector?' he murmured.

'I doubt it,' I replied. 'But it doesn't matter as long as we can get into the building for you to take a look at this ghost.'

'That's actually quite clever,' said the superintendent.

'We women have our uses,' I replied. I would have liked to say more, but Jude was taking us upstairs again.

'Let's try the reading room first,' he said. 'That's where you felt the spirit before.'

Superintendent Hicks gazed about him with a faint smile as we mounted the stairs. 'Oh yes,' he said. 'It's almost exactly as I remember. A few new faces on the walls, of course, but otherwise—'

'Careful!' I cried, as he nearly walked into a couple chatting while they came downstairs.

The reading room was quiet today, with only a couple of people absorbed in their books. Steph made a show of walking slowly around it, pointing her device in various directions. The superintendent didn't accompany her. Instead, he sat down and took in the room. 'Isn't it lovely,' he said. 'I used to spend more time in the newsroom, though. And the dining room. Oh, the food was wonderful.' He shot me a sly glance. 'Not that you'd know, of course.'

I walked over to Inspector Farnsworth and sat beside him, clenching my fists in my lap. 'You're so lucky that you can't see or hear him.'

'I gathered,' murmured the inspector. 'Speaking of seeing or hearing, do you sense anything?'

'Not a thing,' I replied. 'And I assume you don't

either. Superintendent,' I called, 'any sign of a ghost? Apart from us, of course.'

'I'm just preparing myself to investigate,' said the superintendent, leaning back in his chair.

'Nothing from the superintendent,' I told our human colleagues. 'He's having a lovely time reliving his past life.'

Superintendent Hicks glared at me. 'If you wish to find yourself on the wrong end of a disciplinary, Miss Norris, do continue.'

'I report to Inspector Farnsworth, not you,' I replied. 'I suggest we try the newsroom.'

'I'm getting nothing,' said Steph, with a last sweep of her arm. 'Could we try the newsroom, Jude?'

'By all means,' said Jude. Was it my imagination, or did he look weary as he waited for us at the door? I wanted to apologise, but of course there was no point.

We felt the change of atmosphere as soon as Jude opened the newsroom door. A chill hung in the air. 'There may be a problem with the radiators,' he said, but we knew better.

I stayed in the doorway, remembering the nausea I had suffered during the previous encounter. 'You too?' whispered Steph, then walked into the room and beckoned the others.

They walked towards her. 'Oh yes,' said the superintendent. 'There's definitely someone here. Can't see him, but there's a funny smell.' He sniffed once, twice. 'I know that smell, but it's been a long time…'

He followed his nose to one of the large windows facing the street, then pointed to the curtain. Steph hurried over and moved it aside, and several pairs of eyes followed her.

'Gotcha!' cried the superintendent, and made to grab what looked like thin air. 'Damn, he's spry.'

'Who is he?' I asked. 'Do you recognise him?'

'He's familiar, but…' His brow furrowed, and he seemed to follow the progress of something across the room. 'He's very old.'

'How old?' I asked.

'Ninety,' said the superintendent. 'At least.' His frown deepened. 'I'm only saying what I see,' he shouted.

A strong smell, like eau de cologne but stronger, made everyone but Jude recoil. 'Can you sense anything?' he asked the inspector.

'Definitely,' the inspector replied. He pulled out a handkerchief and covered his mouth and nose. 'Jude, would you mind waiting outside? We'd like to contain this if we possibly can, and it may be distressing to watch.'

The struggle between reluctance to leave his post and apprehension about what he might see if he didn't was plain on Jude's face. He was still handsome, though. 'Um, if you wish. I'll be on the landing.

Please do call if you need anything.' He withdrew with a final plaintive glance.

The inspector shut the door. 'Easier to talk when we're alone,' he muttered, moving to a quiet corner. 'What can you see, Superintendent Hicks? Can you describe the ghost? What sort of clothes is he wearing?'

'He's in a suit. A good one, but rusty with wear. Tie with a crest. Might be a university or a regiment. He's got white hair, thin on top, properly short at the back, not touching his collar. I suppose that's something.'

'Any distinctive features?' asked Steph.

'Blue eyes, beaky nose, and an extremely annoying voice.' The superintendent paused. 'Yes it is. And it's a voice I've heard before. Let me think about this.' He sat down at an unoccupied table and put his fingers to his temples.

'You go, Derren Brown,' muttered Steph. It probably made sense to her.

'An old man, known to the superintendent,' said Steph. 'Presumably ninety or so at the time of his death—'

'Bell,' said Superintendent Hicks. His eyes were squeezed shut. 'It's the voice. He was much younger when I knew him, and I didn't know him from here. It was at the police station. Reverend Vexed, my officers used to call him. He came in two or three times a week, complaining of youths throwing stones, or talking too loudly, or loitering where he thought they shouldn't. Criminals of the future, he used to say.' He raised his head. 'Yes, you did,' he shouted. 'Many's the time I had to come out and deal with you because you wouldn't budge until you'd taken it to the top.'

'So this is a Reverend Bell?' said Steph. 'You're absolutely sure?'

'I'm sure as I can be,' said Superintendent Hicks. 'He's a good sixty years older than he was when I knew him, but that kind of voice stays with you. Here, where are you going? Come back!' He stood up, then gasped. 'The cheeky blighter!'

'Don't worry,' said Steph. 'You've identified him, so hopefully we can start to investigate.' She looked considerably happier already. 'Let's go and talk to Jude.'

Inspector Farnsworth sighed. 'I'd feel much better if I knew more than half of what's going on.'

Steph and the inspector led the way, and we met Jude on the landing.

'We've made considerable progress,' said the inspector, and Superintendent Hicks snorted. 'The troubled spirit appears to be an old man, perhaps in his eighties or nineties, wearing a suit, and with tidy white hair. We believe him to be the ghost of a Reverend Bell.'

'Oh my!' Jude stared at him, slack-jawed. 'The

Rev! Father of the club! That's what we call the oldest member,' he added.

'So you know him,' said Inspector Farnsworth.

'Yes. Well, I *knew* him. He'd been a member since the sixties, if you can believe it. He used to come in quite often and sit in the newsroom, reading the papers. He'd talk to anyone who would listen about the amount of crime on the streets and how something ought to be done. Then he'd have his morning coffee and take a little nap. Wouldn't hurt a fly. We saw less of him lately, but I was still shocked when I heard the news of his death.'

'You must have been,' said Steph. 'Can you remember when that was? Was it recent?'

'It was very recent.' Jude leaned forward. 'Is he about?' he whispered.

Steph looked at Superintendent Hicks, who shook his head. 'No, he's gone,' she said.

'In that case… Let me show you.'

Jude took us downstairs and pointed to a noticeboard. There were various notices about awards and prestigious speaking engagements, but Jude pointed to a piece of paper with a black border.

We are sorry to inform you of the death of Member 693, Reverend Norman Bell, on the 1st December. May he rest in peace.

'The first of December,' said Inspector Farnsworth. 'Jude, can you remember when the disturbances began?'

'If you give me a moment, I can check the complaints log.' Jude left us in the hall, and returned two minutes later with a look on his face which mingled shock and incredulity. 'I don't believe this. According to the log, the first complaint was on the second of December. The day after the Rev's death.'

'Well, well,' said Superintendent Hicks, rocking back and forth on the balls of his feet. 'Things are getting interesting.' And much as I would have liked to contradict him, I couldn't disagree.

CHAPTER 5

Jude looked hopeful. 'So . . . you can fix it?'

'It's hard to say,' said Inspector Farnsworth. 'The problem is that he won't speak to us, and he isn't inclined to stay put. Therefore, it's hard to know why he's making mischief.'

'Oh,' said Jude. 'Does that mean we're stuck with him? I mean, it's a bit hard on our members.'

'We'll do everything we can, Jude,' said Steph, and cast a significant glance at where Superintendent Hicks was standing, arms folded.

'I don't know why you're staring at me,' he said. 'In case you've forgotten, I am no longer a serving police officer.'

'Rubbish,' I scoffed. 'If you're no longer part of the Liverpool City Police – I mean Merseyside Police,' I corrected, at a look from Steph – 'then why are you stuck in the Bridewell for eternity?'

'Your guess is as good as mine,' the superintendent

replied. 'However, I'm pretty sure it is not part of my duty as a superintendent to chase errant clerics around a private club. That sort of legwork is for constables.'

'If I could see him, I'd gladly do it,' I snapped. 'Unfortunately, however, he's as big a woman-hater as you are.'

'Look here!' Superintendent Hicks took a step towards me, his face as black as thunder. I quaked, but stood my ground.

'Um, is there anything I can do to help?' Jude asked, and I realised that as far as he was concerned, Inspector Farnsworth and Steph had been standing there silently for the last minute or so.

'Ask him for the use of a room,' I said. 'It's the only way we can hope to get anything done.'

'Yes, Jude, there is,' said the inspector. 'If you could make a room available to us – nothing fancy, a spare office would do – then Constable Sharpe and I can plan our strategy.' Steph held up the black box.

'No problem,' said Jude. If anything, I suspect he was glad of an excuse to shunt us out of view of the club's regulars.

A few minutes later, we were clustered in a small office. It had two chairs, one of which was claimed by Superintendent Hicks, so Steph and I were forced to stand. Jude brought two coffees and a plate of biscuits, which the superintendent kept eyeing. They were about as much use to him as a mirror.

'We have to do something,' Steph said. 'Please, Superintendent Hicks.'

'I'll second that,' said Inspector Farnsworth. 'Even though this chair is comfortable and the coffee is lovely.'

'I am not compromising my position as a senior officer, and that's the end of it,' said the superintendent.

'Fine,' I said. 'Then I'll go. I can't see him, but I can certainly sense him. Maybe I can persuade him to tell us what's going on.'

'You?' The superintendent laughed. 'He won't talk to the likes of you.'

I shrugged. 'Well, you won't talk to the likes of him.' I turned to the inspector. 'Any objections, Inspector Farnsworth?'

'None whatsoever,' said the inspector. 'Since, from what I hear, the superintendent and the reverend don't get on, perhaps a stranger will have better luck with him.'

'I beg your pardon?' Superintendent Hicks spluttered. 'So you intend to cut me out entirely?'

'You cut yourself out,' said Steph. 'Would you like me to come too, Nora, as moral support? I can wave this.' She tapped the black box which was sitting on the desk.

'Yes, please,' I replied. 'If you don't mind me

asking, Steph, what is that? I presume it isn't really a ghost detector.'

Steph grinned. 'It's an infrared tape measure, Nora.' She finished her coffee. 'Let's see what we can find.'

'Good luck, you two,' said Inspector Farnsworth. Superintendent Hicks said nothing.

'It's probably best if I do most of the talking,' I said, as we climbed the stairs. 'I'll pop into each room while you wait outside, and let you know if he's there.'

In turn we visited the newsroom, the reading room, and the dining room, but there was no trace of Reverend Bell. 'Now what do we do?' asked Steph.

'We look elsewhere. Where would a vicar hole up?'

'No idea,' said Steph. 'And if he's somewhere off-limits to the public, I'll have to ask permission.'

I grinned. 'I won't.'

I left the dining room, which was full of enticing smells of no use to a ghost like me, and we strolled downstairs. As we reached the landing, I spied a door opposite the reading room. 'I wonder what's in there?' I put my nose to the glass panel and saw shelves full of books. 'Oooh.'

'What is it?' Steph joined me. 'Move over a bit, will you. Oh, these must be the stacks. Jude mentioned them, remember?' She twisted the knob under the keypad. 'Access denied.'

'Not to me. Stand back, I'm going in.'

It was an effort to get through the thick, heavy door, and it took me a moment to get my bearings. I took a couple of steps forward, and—

'Who goes there?' The speaker was a tall man, only a little transparent, with a pointed brown beard. He was dressed in a suit which tapered at ankles and wrists, cut to accentuate a waist which had thickened since he bought it. 'Where is your pass?'

I wished I had the letter which proclaimed me an officer of the Merseyside police force, but it was in Steph's keeping. 'The concierge said I could come in.'

'That doesn't matter. I am Mr Chapman, the librarian of the Athenaeum, and I need to see authorisation, young lady.'

'I was born in the nineteenth century,' I said. 'Less of the young.'

'No authorisation, no entry.' I suspected Mr Chapman would get on well with Superintendent Hicks.

I decided on a different approach. 'I'm not here to consult your archives. My name is Nora Norris and I am an officer of the Liverpool City Police. I'm looking for Reverend Bell.' As I said the name, a pungent odour drifted through the stacks. 'I have reason to believe that he is here.'

The librarian went to a small desk wedged in the

corner and turned the pages of a large book, bound in green leather, which flickered in and out of view like a lightbulb that was about to blow. 'Norris . . . Norris… You did say Norris, didn't you?'

'I did. But you won't find me there. I'm not a member.'

He closed the book with a satisfied smile. 'No admission for non-members without a pass.'

'I'm pretty sure that once someone dies, they cease to be a member,' I pointed out. 'So Reverend Bell probably shouldn't be in here either.'

'What do you mean?' Mr Chapman's face flushed a shade of red which suggested the probable manner of his end. 'I am still the librarian, no matter what my mortal status, and as far as I'm concerned, the same courtesy extends to *all* members of the Athenaeum.'

Behind him, a book fell to the floor. He jumped, then huffed. 'Please be careful with the books, Reverend Bell.' I could have sworn I heard a faint snigger.

'Reverend Bell!' I called.

'*Quiet* in the library!' thundered the librarian.

'May I speak to you for a moment? It's about the club.'

Three more books hit the floor, and a smell like rotten violets drifted towards me.

'Be quiet, I said! Can't you see what you're doing?'

'I'm trying to help,' I whispered. 'He's causing

trouble in the club. I want to know why, so that we can help him.'

I clapped my hand over my nose and mouth as the smell intensified with a rush of air. 'If the superintendent apologises, I'll speak to him.' The whisper tickled my ear, and somehow it had the tone of a creaking gate. 'Not you.'

I nodded, not trusting myself to open my mouth and speak in case I was sick. I wasn't sure if I could be sick, as a ghost, but I had no intention of finding out.

I backed towards the door. 'Thank you for your help,' I choked out, and squeezed myself through.

'I take it he's in there,' said Steph as I bent over, retching.

'He is, and he's pushing books off the shelves. The librarian isn't at all happy. The ghost librarian.'

'Of course,' said Steph. 'The ghost librarian.'

I ran my tongue around my mouth and swallowed. I longed to go to the dining room and banish the vicar's cologne with the wholesome smells of roasted meat and custard. 'He spoke to me, but only to say that he'd speak to the superintendent if he apologised.'

'Then we're scuppered,' said Steph.

'Not necessarily,' I replied. 'Here's what we'll do…'

A short time later Steph brought me, spluttering

and choking, back to the office. Inspector Farnsworth was reading on his phone, or at least pretending to, while Superintendent Hicks appeared to be having a nap. However, as he opened his eyes immediately on our arrival, I suspected he was putting it on. 'What happened?' he said.

'Nora found Reverend Bell,' said Steph, 'and it didn't go too well.'

'He was in the stacks,' I gasped, 'annoying the librarian. And he spoke to me.'

'He spoke to you?' The superintendent managed to look concerned and indignant all at once. 'What did he say?'

Inspector Farnsworth stood up and offered me his chair. I winked at him with the eye Superintendent Hicks couldn't see and sank into it gratefully. 'He was pushing books – real books – off the shelves.'

'He can't do that.' A noise like a growl came from the superintendent. 'Some of the books here are very valuable.'

'They looked valuable,' I agreed breathlessly. 'He says that he'll speak to you, on one condition.'

Superintendent Hicks moved his chair closer. 'What's that, Nora?'

'He wants you to apologise.'

'Me, apologise? Never! I've done nothing wrong.'

'We know that,' said Steph. 'It wouldn't have to be a real apology. You wouldn't have to mean it.'

Superintendent Hicks frowned so hard that his eyes were mere glittering points beneath his brow. 'I am not apologising.'

I took a deep breath and flung up my head. 'Then I'll have to go back.' I got to my feet and immediately sank down. 'Maybe in a minute or two.'

'Absolutely not, Nora,' said Inspector Farnsworth. 'You're in no fit state to confront this man. I am not letting one of my officers go into potential danger.'

'Of course not,' said Steph. 'Oh, Nora, I'd give you a hug if I could.'

'I know you would,' I said quietly. 'But if it's the only way…' I got to my feet with the aid of the table, letting my hands sink into it an inch or two. 'I'll be fine if I move slowly.'

'No,' said Superintendent Hicks. 'Sit. You're my officer too.' He stood up, tugged down his jacket and adjusted his tie. 'I shall go, as the senior officer. And none of you are to try and stop me.'

'Are you sure?' asked Steph. 'I mean, Nora's young and fit—'

'How dare you!' Superintendent Hicks shouted.

Inspector Farnsworth jumped, and stared straight at him. 'Um, hello, Superintendent. Nice to see you at last.'

But Superintendent Hicks was too busy dealing with Steph. 'What you just said is insubordination, Constable Sharpe. When I have finished with

Reverend Bell, I shall return and deal with you.' He let out a snort very like one of Prince's, then turned to the inspector. 'Farnsworth, come with me to the library. We must deal with this man before he does any more damage.'

'Right you are, Superintendent,' said Inspector Farnsworth. 'If you would lead the way?'

'I'd be delighted,' said Superintendent Hicks, striding through the door as if it wasn't there. Inspector Farnsworth grinned at us as he opened it.

'Farnsworth! I haven't got all day!' bellowed the superintendent. And as the inspector's footsteps receded, Steph and I made our best attempt at a high-five.

CHAPTER 6

A few minutes later, we were surprised by Inspector Farnsworth's return. We both jumped out of our seats, then saw his expression.

'What's up, sir?' asked Steph. 'The Rev hasn't gone to ground, has he?'

'Not yet,' said Inspector Farnsworth, gloomily. 'Although I can't hear or see him. The superintendent isn't the most diplomatic of people.'

'You're telling me,' I replied.

'I'm only getting one side of it,' said the inspector, 'but I have the distinct feeling that it isn't going well.'

'And...?' asked Steph, with a hopeful expression on her face.

'And I wondered if Nora would care to join us. I'd invite you too, Steph, but I'd rather not overwhelm the poor man. We could say that you're our . . . welfare officer, Nora. Yes.' He seemed pleased with this, and I have to say that I didn't mind either.

'I could come too,' said Steph, 'in case I'm needed. If he doesn't want me there, he can always say.'

Inspector Farnsworth sighed. 'You know what I said about overwhelming him? Let's try with Nora first and see what happens.'

'I'll come up and wait,' Steph said firmly.

I admired her persistence as we trailed upstairs to the library, stuck behind two men who were talking about politics. Jude was waiting outside the door, looking both concerned and puzzled. 'Is everything all right, Inspector?'

'Yes, thank you,' said Inspector Farnsworth. 'I was, um, checking something downstairs. Steph, if you wouldn't mind passing me the apparatus.'

Steph put the tape measure in his hand.

'Thank you.' Jude opened the door, and I waited for the inspector to go in, in case he needed to make introductions. I noticed as I passed Jude that he didn't react to my presence. I would have heaved a sigh if there had been any point.

But as soon as I entered the room, my attention was riveted by a stand-up argument.

'Explain the reason for your disgraceful behaviour!' thundered Superintendent Hicks. 'You, a man of the cloth, causing a disturbance. And worse, damaging books!'

'I wouldn't expect you to understand,

Superintendent,' the Rev replied, and oh, the sneer in his voice. 'Only a member would understand.'

'I've visited the Athenaeum many times, I'll have you know.' In my imagination, the superintendent was probably emphasising each word with a jab of his finger.

Inspector Farnsworth walked forward, passing the admission desk and the first few rows of shelves. I wondered where Mr Chapman had got to. Perhaps he had given up on any peace and quiet and retreated elsewhere. At any rate, there the two of them were, red-faced and practically snorting steam.

'Gentlemen,' said the inspector.

They both glared at him.

'Things are getting heated, so I've brought our welfare officer to see you, Reverend Bell.'

I cleared my throat and Inspector Farnsworth looked at me. 'If you wish to speak to the reverend,' I said, 'he's standing in front of that shelf full of green books.'

'Oh, sorry.' The inspector faced where I had indicated. 'So you can see him, Sergeant Norris?'

I practically choked. Sergeant Norris! I knew it was only to impress the Rev, but even so… I stored that away to tease Steph with later. 'Yes, Inspector, I can.' I took a step forward. 'Reverend, it's a pleasure to meet you. I'm Sergeant Norris, an officer of the Merseyside Police with particular responsibility for spiritual welfare.' Out of the corner of my eye I saw Superintendent Hicks goggling at me, and did my best to ignore him. 'You appear cross. Can I help?'

'I doubt it,' snapped the Rev. 'But you can't be worse than him.' He jerked a thumb at the superintendent, who was opening and shutting his mouth like a fish on the dockside.

'I'll do my best,' I said, taking another step forward, and in the process getting the superintendent out of my sight line. 'What seems to be the problem?'

'There is no seems about it! How would you like it if you had to share your home with an utter oik?'

I thought of the various officers who came to the Bridewell and spent their time eating takeaways and playing games on their phones. 'That must be terrible,' I replied. 'So there's someone here you don't get along with.'

'Get along with?' He looked ready to explode. 'You make it sound as if it's no more than liking different football teams! The man's pure evil – I can sense it!'

Inspector Farnsworth nudged me. 'Can you ask him if this is a ghost or a person who is currently alive?' he murmured.

'I don't know why he doesn't just speak to me,' said Reverend Bell. 'I'm right here.'

'I'm afraid the inspector can't see or hear you. But he does ask good questions.'

'Thank you, Nora,' said Inspector Farnsworth.

'All right, you two,' said the Rev. 'No, he's not alive, and there's no way on God's earth that he could ever be a member of the Athenaeum.'

'How do you know that, Reverend?' I asked. 'Is he someone you knew . . . before?'

'How dare you!' The Rev took a step towards me, and despite his old bones, I took a step back.

'No threatening our officers,' said Superintendent Hicks, putting himself between me and Reverend Bell. 'Or there will be trouble.' I wasn't sure what sort of trouble he meant, but he seemed confident that there would be, and I suppose that was the main thing. 'Answer the question, please.'

'I can see I shall have to spell this out,' said the Rev, speaking as if to a small child. 'The man couldn't possibly be a member because he is so shabbily dressed. I've never seen him in the newsroom or the reading room, or indeed in here. He just wanders around downstairs. He probably can't even read. I have no idea how he sneaked in, and I want him removed.'

'Ah,' I said. 'Could you tell us a bit more about him, Reverend? Do you know his name?'

'Of course not! Do you think I would lower myself to speak to someone like that? You ask him, if you're so keen to have a conversation with the lout.'

'I'm afraid we haven't seen him as yet. Could you

describe him, and we'll keep a look out.'

'Very well,' said the Rev. 'Get your flesh-and-blood person to make notes.'

I turned to Inspector Farnsworth. 'Inspector, the reverend has asked whether you would mind writing down a description. I'll relay it to you.'

'Certainly,' said the inspector, taking out his notebook.

'Well trained, isn't he,' said the Rev.

I decided not to pass that on. 'If you'll begin, Reverend.'

'He's a villainous-looking man. In his thirties or thereabouts, scruffy and unshaven. Brown hair that needs a cut. He's probably infested with lice, come to think of it. Clothes of the poorest, and work boots.'

'He's a working man in his thirties,' I told the inspector. 'Possibly quite poor.' I faced the Rev. 'When might he have lived? And does he have any distinguishing marks?'

'He's got a tattoo on each hand. Three stars on his left hand and something like a snake on his right. Tattoos, in the Athenaeum! As for when he comes from, his clothes are ancient. Corduroy trousers, a dirty shirt with no collar, and a waistcoat with half the buttons missing. There's a watch chain goes across it, but I'd lay money there's no watch on the end.'

I relayed this to the inspector. 'When you say he looks villainous, what do you mean? Can you describe his face?'

'Don't know what he started out like,' said the Rev, 'but he's been punched enough times that most of it's been rearranged. Broken nose, scar running through his eyebrow, and barely teeth to eat a piece of bread with. Between that and his accent, which is as thick as sea fog, I can scarcely make out a word he says. But it's the evil air that hangs around him, that's what you want to look out for. Whatever he did, it was horrible. The sort of thing you can't escape. Get him out of here, and bring him to justice however you can. Then I'll be able to sleep easy.'

'We'll do our best,' I said. 'Thank you very much for your time, Reverend Bell. We'll go to our office and continue investigating.'

'Good,' he said. 'At least someone's doing something.' He gave Superintendent Hicks a contemptuous look and the superintendent's fists clenched.

'Time to go,' I sang out. Once my back was turned to the Rev, I glanced at Superintendent Hicks and motioned towards the door. He stalked through it and I followed.

'How do you think—'

'I'm not talking about it till I'm away from that man,' muttered the superintendent.

Shortly afterwards, we were back in our ground-floor office. I wondered if the spirit who had annoyed the Rev so much would pop in to say hello. I hoped he would. I suspected the Rev's dislike for him was based on his class rather than his character.

Inspector Farnsworth took out his notebook and sighed. 'Did the Rev say anything else useful, Nora?'

I repeated the Rev's comments on the spirit's appearance in as impersonal a manner as I could.

'How do we find him without a name?' asked Steph.

I shrugged. 'I don't know. He doesn't sound like someone who'd be a member, so he won't be on the books.'

'Those tattoos, though...' said Inspector Farnsworth. 'If he has a criminal record, we could try the Digital Panopticon.'

'The what?' said Steph, which was exactly what I was thinking.

'It's a searchable database of information about people who went on trial in the Old Bailey, in London,' said Inspector Farnsworth. 'I have an interest in the history of criminology, you see. And while the Panopticon is London-focused, it's the only resource I can think of which captures things like tattoos.'

'Oh,' I said, none the wiser.

'We can search the database with what Reverend Bell has told us and look for a match. Those tattoos are distinctive, we have a physical description, and presumably the man was born in Liverpool, which narrows things down.'

'In that case, let's go there.'

Inspector Farnsworth stared at me. 'Go where?'

'This panopticon place. Is it in London? Do you need to pack?'

He laughed. 'No, Nora, it's an online database. I can use it on my phone. Look.' He took out his dratted phone and started tapping at it. A few seconds later, he showed me the screen. At the top it said *Digital Panopticon*. 'And now we search.'

I leaned against the wall and folded my arms. Was there anything these calculator things couldn't do? Did police officers even go out on the beat any more, or feel anyone's collar? I glanced at Superintendent Hicks who was sitting on the other chair, knees apart and arms folded. I suspected he felt much as I did.

'Here we go,' said Inspector Farnsworth, a minute later. 'John Finley, also known as Jack Finley. Born 1860, Liverpool. Tattoos on both hands matching the Rev's description. Broken nose, scar on eyebrow, brown hair. Convicted of various crimes in London, including fighting, drunkenness, and simple larceny.'

'So he was a thief,' said Superintendent Hicks. 'When did his crimes take place?'

'All in the early 1890s,' the inspector replied. 'So Reverend Bell couldn't possibly have known him.'

'And if he was in his mid-thirties when he died…'

I frowned as I tried to work out where I was going. 'This building wouldn't have been here.'

'What was here before?' asked Steph.

'A church, I believe,' said the inspector. 'Hence Church Alley and Church Street. Let me take a screenshot of Finley's record, and I'll look it up.'

'No need,' I said. 'It was St Peter's Church.'

'In that case, maybe he was buried in the churchyard,' said Steph.

'Good point,' said Inspector Farnsworth, beaming. He tapped at his phone, then shook his head. 'The last burial recorded at St Peter's Church was in 1853.'

We thought this over. Superintendent Hicks was first to break the silence. 'So what is he doing here?'

CHAPTER 7

Inspector Farnsworth shook his head. 'We don't know. How can we? We need more information about the man.'

'We know where he'll be,' I said. 'The Rev told us he stays downstairs. Maybe if we look around, we'll see him.'

'Good idea, Nora,' said Superintendent Hicks. 'Come along, then.'

'Is that a good idea?' asked Steph, and we stared at her. 'I mean, from his record, the last thing he'll want to do is talk to a bunch of police officers. Maybe that's why we haven't seen him yet.'

'Good point,' said Inspector Farnsworth. 'Well, Superintendent Hicks and I aren't in uniform.' He eyed me. 'Nora, is it possible for you to remove your jacket and hat?'

'I don't know.' I'd never tried. My uniform was as much a part of me as my nose or my ears.

I lifted off my hat and laid it on the table. So far, so good. The jacket came next. My fingers slipped on the buttons in my nervousness, but at last it was off and neatly folded on the table. I felt half naked. 'This is . . . strange.'

'It won't be for long,' said Steph. 'I should stay here. He's probably not ready for a conversation with a woman in trousers.' She seemed relieved. I wondered why, then thought of what the Rev had said. *Pure evil...* A little shiver went through me, which was ridiculous. As if a ghost could feel the cold.

'Let's go ghost hunting, then,' said the inspector, and the slight quiver in his voice told me that he wasn't looking forward to it either. 'Actually, before we do, we should tell Jude what we're doing. Apart from anything else, we may need him to let us into some of the rooms.'

Jude was in a little cubbyhole near the front door. Inspector Farnsworth knocked, and he looked up from his screen. Honestly, screens everywhere. 'How are things progressing?' he asked.

'We're getting somewhere,' said Inspector Farnsworth. 'We've managed to communicate with Reverend Bell, and we know what the problem is.'

Jude's face lit up. 'Wonderful! So does that mean he'll give us no more trouble? Or will you exorcise him?'

'Heavens, no,' the inspector said, and Jude's

eyebrows lifted. 'We need to solve the problem. Unfortunately, that involves another spirit who roams on the ground floor of the building.'

'Oh!' Jude considered this. 'So is that the one who's causing the problems? Although if it's downstairs…'

'No, it's not him. Reverend Bell wants him to go away. That's why he's causing a disturbance.'

'I don't follow,' said Jude.

'It's complicated,' said the inspector. 'That's why we specialise in these things. What we've come to ask is whether you would mind showing us – me – around the rooms downstairs.'

'Of course,' said Jude, standing up and taking a large ring of keys from the drawer. Then he looked at Inspector Farnsworth in puzzlement. 'Won't you need your – your ghost apparatus? And isn't Constable Sharpe coming with us?'

'Constable Sharpe is writing up a report on our progress so far,' Inspector Farnsworth replied at once, and I reflected that perhaps that was why he was an inspector. 'But yes, I shall fetch the detector.'

'Doubt you'll need it,' said Superintendent Hicks. 'We'll follow the scent of pure evil.' There was a glint in his eye, and I got the impression that he was very much looking forward to meeting with John Finley.

Tape measure in hand, the inspector and Jude set off together, and Superintendent Hicks and I walked behind them. The superintendent was restless and fidgety, but I was glad not to be at the forefront of the action.

As it worked out, though, I needn't have worried. There was no sign of John Finley anywhere. Neither I nor Superintendent Hicks could see, feel, or hear any trace of him.

We inspected each room. There was a beautiful meeting room, and even the service areas were well-equipped, bright and clean. I remembered the house I had grown up in, cramped, sooty and dirty, despite our best efforts to keep it clean, and felt a pang of resentment. *People today don't know how lucky they are.* That served to distract me from the purpose of our mission. But in any case, it had failed.

Jude kept glancing at the tape measure as if it were a ticking bomb, and asking Inspector Farnsworth if it was picking anything up.

'No,' Superintendent Hicks and I would chorus.

'I'm afraid not,' said the inspector, and off we went to the next room.

Soon, we were out of rooms. 'What is the best course of action now, Inspector?' asked Jude.

'This case is more complex than I initially thought,' said Inspector Farnsworth. 'I think the best thing to do is compare notes with Constable Sharpe, but we can do that at the station.'

'What about the Rev?' I asked. 'What do we tell

him? We need to say something, or he might carry on causing trouble. And damaging books.' To be honest, it was the damaged books that bothered me most.

'Before we leave,' Inspector Farnsworth continued, 'could I visit the library once more?'

'No problem at all,' said Jude, and while he was perfectly polite, I got the impression that he was rather tired of us.

I was tired of the situation too, and I'm afraid I didn't wait for Jude and the inspector. 'Come on,' I said to Superintendent Hicks, and mounted the stairs ahead of them. We were in the library before our living companions had reached the landing.

Reverend Bell was sitting with Mr Chapman, haranguing him, but he broke off when he saw us. 'Have you dealt with him?' he asked.

'We've made considerable progress,' I said, taking a leaf out of Inspector Farnsworth's book. 'We know who he is, when he lived, and some of what he did, but we need to do more research. From what you have said, he is a dangerous individual whom we must approach carefully.'

The Rev's eyebrows lowered.

'What you said about pure evil impressed us greatly,' I continued, widening my eyes and looking as innocent as I could. 'We treat complaints from our – our spiritual clients with the utmost seriousness. We don't treat any complaint lightly.'

'I should think not,' said the Rev, with a harrumph.

'So if we could ask you to refrain from making your displeasure felt, we shall continue to work on the case and keep you up to date on any developments.' I sensed Superintendent Hicks twitching at my side, desperate to speak.

'Hmm. Well.' The Rev thought this over.

'That will allow us to concentrate our efforts on finding and dealing with this spirit. I know that's what you want us to do.'

'Yes, indeed. Go on then, get to it.' The Rev turned to the librarian. 'I still prefer the second edition of Newman's *Parochial and Plain Sermons*. In my opinion, you made the wrong choice.'

The door of the library opened as we were about to leave. 'Don't do anything,' I muttered to Inspector Farnsworth, and his face fell. 'I've dealt with the Rev. Wave the tape measure and look at a couple of books. We'll see you downstairs.'

While we waited for Inspector Farnsworth's return, we told Steph what had happened – or not happened.

'So you didn't sense him anywhere?' she said. 'Are you sure you checked every room?'

'We went round with Jude, Steph,' I replied, as I put my jacket on. 'I'm sure he showed us everything. Just because you weren't there, that doesn't mean we didn't do a good job.'

'I didn't say that.'

'You implied it, Constable Sharpe,' said the superintendent. 'And I didn't like your tone.'

'Oh, come on,' said Steph. 'I ask one question—'

'It's the way you asked it,' I said, thoroughly nettled. 'As if we wouldn't know what to do.' I jammed my hat on my head. 'Seeing as I worked out that we needed the superintendent, and I've persuaded the Rev not to cause any more trouble, then if anyone's the spare part, it's you.'

The minute the words were out, I regretted it. Steph looked at me, and I could tell she was working out what to say.

I opened my mouth to say sorry as Inspector Farnsworth came in and tossed the tape measure on the table. 'Right, I've carried out my orders. Let's go. Some of us have work to do.'

We all glared at him. 'We're only here because you invited us, Inspector,' I said.

'True.' He sighed. 'Sorry. It's just . . . frustrating. Anyway, sitting in here won't help and I have a meeting in half an hour, not to mention a desk-full of paperwork. I'll drop you off on the way.'

We trailed after him, perhaps more slowly than we needed to, though I was glad to see the back of the place and I suspected the others felt the same. Inspector Farnsworth and Steph said their farewells to Jude, promising to keep him informed of developments, and we walked to the police car in silence.

Steph was about to open the back door when Superintendent Hicks spoke. 'I'll sit with Nora. You two can travel in the front.' The tone of his voice indicated not that he was doing them a favour, but that they deserved each other.

'What do we do now?' asked Steph, as the car moved off.

'I need to concentrate,' said Inspector Farnsworth. 'The roads are surprisingly busy at this time.'

'I could check the files at the Bridewell,' said Steph. 'And any other records from the time that we can find. See if we can find out more about John Finley.'

'Yes, I suppose,' said the inspector. 'Yes, do that.'

'What do *we* do?' I asked. 'The superintendent and me?'

There was a pause. 'You could tell us where the files are located,' said Steph.

While I probably deserved that after my outburst, I still wasn't impressed. I rolled my eyes at the superintendent, who shrugged. He took his pipe from his pocket, and for the rest of the journey he surrounded himself with a near-impenetrable cloud of smoke while I brooded, too wrapped up in my own feelings even to enjoy Liverpool speeding past.

CHAPTER 8

I was relieved when Inspector Farnsworth pulled up outside the Bridewell. I wanted to be away from people for a while – both ghost and mortal.

'I'll be tied up for the rest of the day,' said the inspector, and for a moment I imagined him bound to a chair. Then again, that probably wasn't too far from the truth. 'I'll try and look in tomorrow, but don't count on it.'

'OK, sir.' Steph released her seatbelt, which retracted with a click and a whoosh. 'I'll write up what I can on the laptop. Shall I email you a copy?'

'Best not,' said the inspector. 'Probably better that we don't discuss this on the official systems. Anyway, I must get on.'

Steph got out. 'Bye, sir,' she said, and closed the door. Then she checked no one was near enough to see and opened our door. 'Come on, you two.' Her tone was – not unfriendly, but brisk. Giving an order rather than offering encouragement.

Superintendent Hicks took his time getting out, and Steph huffed. I followed at a reasonable speed. As soon as the rear door was closed, the car moved off.

'Someone's in a hurry,' said Superintendent Hicks.

'Well, yes,' said Steph. 'He's got meetings and places to be.'

'Lucky him.' And we followed Steph into the Bridewell.

'I might visit Prince,' I said. 'I bet he's missed me.'

'That can wait, Nora,' said Steph. 'First, I need you to come to the file room and show me where to find the right records.'

'Don't you know?' I countered. 'I thought you'd have done those already.'

'As it happens, no,' said Steph. 'I began at 1915, as that was roughly when you started working here. I wasn't told to begin at the beginning.'

'Bet you wish you had now,' I said, as we went downstairs. 'Anyway, when is the beginning?'

'The station was built in 1846,' Superintendent Hicks declared, behind us. 'However, we can assume that John Finley died before he was forty, which narrows things down.'

'Marginally,' replied Steph, glancing round.

'Watch out!' I cried. 'The hole!'

'Wha—' Steph stumbled, avoiding it by a whisker.

'Do look where you're going,' I said. 'You could

have broken your ankle.'

'If people weren't distracting me…'

'A thank you wouldn't hurt,' I shot back.

'Thank you,' she said, not looking remotely thankful. 'Let's get to the file room and talk there.'

The file room seemed darker and dingier than ever after the splendour of the Athenaeum. 'Where should I be looking, then?' said Steph.

'As I *said*,' boomed Superintendent Hicks, 'this Finley character was almost certainly no more than forty when he died. If he was born in 1860, the earliest date to look for him here is 1875 or so.'

'Fine, I'll take your word for it,' said Steph. '1875 it is.'

Superintendent Hicks pointed to the fifth cabinet along from the door. 'You start there.'

'Right.' Steph opened the top drawer of the cabinet and walked her fingers through the files. '1873 . . . 1874…' She closed the drawer and opened the next one down. 'Still 1874… OK, 1875.' She pulled out a fat wodge of files. 'Actually, I could enter these on the laptop too. That will kill two birds with one stone.'

'Maybe Inspector Farnsworth will give you a house point,' I said.

Steph looked at me, her face expressionless. 'Maybe he will,' she said, at last. She took her laptop out of its bag and put it on the table. 'I'm making a drink.' She left the room and her footsteps grew fainter, with a creak or two as she went upstairs.

Superintendent Hicks and I exchanged glances. 'Do you want to stay?' I asked him.

'Not particularly. I mean, it's not as if we can do anything. She wanted us to tell her where the files were, and that's done. I consider that we have performed our duty admirably today.'

'Me too. Let's go to the yard, get some air. It always feels so stuffy in here.'

'After you,' said the superintendent, and we walked through the door. 'In any case, if Constable Sharpe did require our help, it's not as if we're difficult to find, is it?'

'Exactly.'

We went upstairs, then down the corridor, and soon we were outside, under grey clouds. Prince wasn't there – presumably he was in what had been his stable, where I didn't like to go. I dreaded being in a small space with a horse who might kick.

However, Queen Vic, a small, stout horse who would have been black if she was fully there, roamed the yard, scraping her hoof on the cobbles and occasionally bending to take a mouthful of whatever stubby grass had poked through in her day.

I walked slowly towards her. 'Hello.'

Queen Vic raised her head and regarded me with incurious dark-amber eyes.

Superintendent Hicks ambled up to her and

stroked her nose. 'What do you make of it, Nora?'

'I wonder if she's more transparent than Prince because I've spent less time with her,' I said. 'I don't know how it works.'

That made him chuckle. 'I meant the case.'

I shrugged. 'It probably isn't my place to say. Steph made it pretty clear earlier that we're more or less making up the numbers.'

The superintendent snorted. 'That's rich. Without us, they'd have got precisely nowhere.'

'We both know that,' I replied, my resentment rising. '*They* don't. Too busy messing about on their phones. No doubt Inspector Farnsworth thinks he'll be able to solve the case from his armchair.'

'I wouldn't put it past him,' said the superintendent. 'I only showed myself to him so that we could get the Rev to talk, after he affected you so badly.'

'What? Oh, yes.' I remembered my subterfuge from earlier and was thankful that as far as I knew, I could no longer blush. 'Thank you for that, Superintendent Hicks.'

'Think nothing of it. You were very brave.'

'I was. And I was a sergeant, too. For all of ten minutes.'

'Funny, isn't it.' The superintendent took out his pipe. 'All the praise when there's something only we can do, and the minute it's completed, back in our box we go.'

'That's exactly it,' I said. 'I bet if you and I had their advantages – being able to travel and talk properly to people, and tap on those stupid phone calculators – we'd have solved this case already.'

'I wouldn't bet against you.' Superintendent Hicks began to fill his pipe. 'But unfortunately, we haven't. So we'll have to lump it when they take the glory for themselves.'

'We don't have to like it, though.' I walked up to Queen Vic and patted her shoulder. She stared at me. I took a step back in case I'd gone too far.

Time passed in the yard. Clouds scudded overhead, the superintendent smoked, darkness fell, and I improved my acquaintance with Queen Vic.

'Here comes trouble,' muttered Superintendent Hicks, and I paused in plaiting Queen Vic's mane to see Steph approaching. She looked tired and there was a faint smudge of dirt on her cheek.

'Thanks for sticking around,' she said, and sneezed.

'Bless you,' I said, as she fumbled for a tissue. Her hands and the tip of her nose were red. 'There wasn't much we could do.'

'It would have been nice to have someone to talk to.'

'We've talked to people all day,' I replied. 'We needed a break. Going to a new place, dealing with the Rev, working out what to do… It's tiring.'

'I'm tired too,' Steph snapped. 'It doesn't stop me doing my job.'

'Yes, but your job ends at half past five. You can go home, or go to the cinema, or have dinner, or talk to Tasha. We're stuck here with nothing to do.'

Steph sighed. 'Is that what this is about? You're jealous of me because I'm alive?'

'Maybe I am,' I said. 'I never got the opportunities you have, and frankly, I don't think you appreciate them.'

'Well, sorry for breathing,' said Steph. 'Oh, um, I didn't mean it like that.'

'It's just frustrating. You and the inspector can drive and find things on your magic phone devices and get yourselves into places, and we can't do a thing without you.'

'We can't do much without you,' said Steph. 'We're dependent on the goodwill of spirits to be able even to see them, half the time.' She pushed her hair back from her forehead, leaving another dusty smudge. 'What we're both saying is that we're frustrated and we need each other's help. And that's all right. Because unless we work together and stop bickering, we won't be able to solve this case. The Rev will carry on being a pain in the neck, and we'll never find this John Finley guy or work out what he's done.'

'She's right,' said Superintendent Hicks, and Queen Vic harrumphed. 'It may not be what any of us want to do, but for the sake of the case we have to work together.'

I sighed. 'I suppose. We're still police officers, and we must do our duty.'

'High five?' asked Steph.

'High what?' said Superintendent Hicks.

'We can't shake hands,' I said. 'This is easier.' I raised my hand and Steph and I demonstrated.

'Is this what modern people do?' He looked disgusted.

'Some do,' said Steph. 'Come on, give it a go.'

Superintendent Hicks held out his hand. Steph brought hers close and mimed high-fiving it. 'There,' she said. Then she took out her phone and climbed halfway up the metal staircase that led to the superintendent's quarters.

'What are you doing?' asked Superintendent Hicks. 'Are you conveying a message to the inspector?'

Steph looked rather embarrassed. 'He'll still be busy, so I'm texting Tasha to see if she fancies a movie after work. I could do with an escape from reality for a couple of hours.'

'Couldn't we all,' said the superintendent. 'Very well, Constable Sharpe. I shall allow you to use your device for a non-work purpose, providing you meet one condition.'

Steph raised her eyebrows. 'Which is?'

Superintendent Hicks smiled. 'Tomorrow you will be required to describe to us the plot of the film, plus any car chases or special effects.'

'You're on.' Steph typed rapidly, then put her phone in her pocket and descended. When she was at the bottom, we heard a buzz. She took the phone out and grinned. 'It's happening. *The Fast and the Furious*, whatever number this one is.'

'Good for you,' I said. 'Make sure you wash your face and hands before you meet Tasha. You're very dusty.'

'Will do,' said Steph. 'See you tomorrow!' She hurried into the station.

'Peace is restored,' said Superintendent Hicks, as the door closed. 'For now, at any rate. I shall retire to my quarters.' He gave Queen Vic a final pat and walked slowly up the metal stairs.

I stayed where I was, feeling as if the spell might break if I left Queen Vic and went into the building. 'We have to try,' I whispered into Queen Vic's mane, and she neighed in agreement. 'It's the only way.'

CHAPTER 9

Superintendent Hicks and I were already in the file room when Steph came in the next morning. The clock said she was ten minutes late. 'I wondered where you two were,' she said, as she put down her mug. But her tone was mild.

'Likewise,' said the superintendent. 'And you didn't have to wonder. We agreed it yesterday, and my word is my bond.' He sat up straight in his seat and regarded Steph with one of his most pompous looks.

'How was the cinema?' I asked. 'Did you enjoy the film?'

'Oh yes.' A dreamy expression came over Steph's face. 'It was… Yes, it was great.' She took a Snickers bar out of her pocket and put it beside the mug.

'Details?' prompted the superintendent.

Steph's eyebrows shot up. 'Really?'

'Yes. You said you'd tell us what happened in the film, remember?'

'Oh yes. Well, there were car chases . . . and a race . . . and there was a bomb.'

'Did anyone drive through a street market?' asked the superintendent. 'Or up a ramp? Or jump over a broken bridge?'

'Um, I don't think so. It was brilliant, though.'

Superintendent Hicks glowered at Steph. 'Frankly, Constable Sharpe, I expected more detail. From the sound of it, you barely paid any attention to what was going on.'

Steph giggled, which made me stare. I would never have had Steph down as a giggler. 'Oh, I definitely paid attention in the cinema. I'll tell you more later. I ought to get on.' She unzipped her laptop bag and went to the filing cabinet.

Superintendent Hicks and I watched Steph go through file after file. Mostly she was silent, with an occasional murmur of 'Drunkenness again', 'Another shoplifter', or 'Who's stupid enough to punch somebody in the middle of a busy street?'

'I take it you haven't found him yet,' I said.

'Nope,' said Steph, tossing her last file on the pile. She stood up, took them to the filing cabinet and retrieved another stack. 'I could be here for months doing this, and find nothing. There has to be a better way.' Her good humour had vanished completely.

'To be honest, I'm not surprised you've drawn a blank,' said Superintendent Hicks. 'The Bridewell has always been more of a lock-up than a main station.'

Steph sighed. 'I gathered. Tell me, you two, what's the most serious case you ever dealt with?'

'No point asking me,' I said. 'I was never involved in any of the serious stuff. I looked after the women and children.'

'Except when you sneaked upstairs to eavesdrop on the detectives,' remarked the superintendent.

'Who were mostly discussing the football or the cricket scores, depending on the season,' I retorted.

He scowled at me. 'Because we were efficient and we got our work done. Unlike some people.'

Steph rolled her eyes. 'Working together, remember?'

Reluctantly, we turned to her. 'It depends how you define serious,' said Superintendent Hicks. 'We uncovered a large-scale protection racket. Shopkeepers were paying a local gang ridiculous sums so that their businesses wouldn't be attacked. That was a bad do.'

'OK, that's something,' said Steph. 'I don't suppose it happened during the period I'm looking at?'

'No, that was much later,' said the superintendent. 'When I started in the force, people watched out for each other. Everyone knew their neighbour's business, and if there were any new people in the area, we kept an eye on them.'

'That isn't very friendly,' said Steph.

'Just taking care of the neighbourhood. Let me think...' Superintendent Hicks put his elbows on the table and rested his chin on his hand. 'Mind if I smoke?'

'Yes,' said Steph. 'It's illegal indoors, in a public place.'

'It won't hurt you,' he replied. 'Or us. We're long past that.'

'The answer's still no,' said Steph. 'We have to set an example.'

The superintendent pouted, then a faraway look came into his eyes. 'We did have the occasional murder.'

'Now we're getting somewhere!' cried Steph.

The superintendent held up a hand. 'Not so fast, Constable Sharpe. The thing is, they were usually heat-of-the-moment affairs. A lot of them were manslaughter, in the end. A man comes home early from work and discovers that his wife isn't, ahem, alone. He drags the chap outside and punches him, the chap hits back, someone's head hits the pavement and they never get up. Crimes of passion.'

Steph considered this. 'What happened in those cases?'

'Well, we brought them in, obviously, but they didn't stay here. As I said, we were more of an overnight lock-up than a proper station. Sometimes we had to boot a regular out of their cell if a real bad case came in.' He smiled. 'They used to be quite aggrieved that they wouldn't get their soup at night and their tea and toast in the morning. Said it was against their rights.'

'So what *happened*?' asked Steph. Bless her, she was trying hard to be patient.

'Don't rush me,' said Superintendent Hicks. 'I'm reminiscing. I don't expect a whippersnapper like you to understand, but I've got a lot of memories to work through.'

'Sorry,' said Steph. She sat back and folded her arms. 'I'll wait, shall I?'

'You could always carry on with those files while you're waiting,' I suggested, and she gave me a filthy look.

'So, the bad cases,' said the superintendent. 'If something like that came up, we'd do the necessary – question the suspect, interview witnesses, talk to the victim if they were still alive. Once we'd ticked all the boxes, we'd knock on the superintendent's door and explain the situation. Then he'd take the file and contact Walton Jail to come and collect our criminal. That was reasonable: after all, they couldn't stay here. We didn't have room, not with our few cells. So we knew we'd be saying goodbye to them. Ninety-nine times out of a hundred, that was the end of it.'

'So the files on serious crimes wouldn't be here,'

said Steph. 'They'd be at the prison. Assuming they haven't been shredded.'

'As far as I know,' said Superintendent Hicks. 'Our superintendent at the time wouldn't have wanted lots of paper cluttering his office. And the family's maid, Gladys, was an absolute dragon. The superintendent was terrified of her.'

'So there's no reason for me to check these at all,' said Steph, gathering the files and taking them to the cabinet. 'What we should be doing is talking to Adam, the historian at HMP Liverpool. If anyone can tell us more about John Finley, it's him.'

'I agree,' said the superintendent. 'We've got no evidence that John Finley was even in the neighbourhood that the Bridewell covers. Liverpool was a sizeable city then, too. It makes much more sense to go straight to the place where serious criminals would be gathered. If we'll find news of John Finley anywhere, it's there.'

A shudder went through me, and I realised how lucky I had been to spend my short police career at a place like the Bridewell. That wasn't to say that it had been easy. I had seen many hard things. I had looked after women taken up for soliciting because they had no other way to earn a crust, or had been forced into it. I did the best I could, fed them well – and their children, who usually came too as there was no one else at home – but I knew once they were released they would be out on the streets again, poor things. I had seen poverty: families scraping by on next to nothing, desperate to stay out of the workhouse where they would most likely be separated.

However, I had also seen kindness and charity: especially from my fellow officers, who regularly brought in vagrants and beggars and gave them a hot meal and a bed for the night. I had never had to face a serious criminal, and the thought that I might have to now made my stomach do things it had not done in a hundred years.

'So we go to the prison,' said Steph. 'That's the obvious next step.'

Superintendent Hicks wagged a finger. 'No, Constable Sharpe. Your obvious next step is to inform Inspector Farnsworth of our conversation and ask his permission to visit the prison.' He tutted. 'You young people, charging off like a bull at a gate.'

'Well, yeah,' said Steph. She took her phone out of her pocket, read something on the screen, smiled, and put it away. 'I'll walk round to Erskine Street station and see if he's in.'

'Why not use your phone?' I asked. 'That would be much quicker. Anyway, he may not be in.'

'You know how bad the reception is,' said Steph. 'I wouldn't want to be cut off halfway through the conversation.' She closed her laptop and stood up. She didn't seem to be in the room with us any more.

'You will take us to the prison, won't you?' said Superintendent Hicks. 'All working together, remember.'

'Of course. Won't be long.' Steph shrugged on her jacket, drained her mug, and hurried off. Her phone was out of her pocket already.

'I can't make Steph out,' I said. 'They're so proud of those phone things and what they can do, so why wouldn't she use it? Reception, whatever that is, has never bothered her before. She just goes up the metal stairs in the yard and gets on with it.'

Superintendent Hicks looked very wise. 'Sometimes, Nora, what's a mystery to one person is crystal clear to another.'

I stared at him. 'What? What mystery? I think it's odd, that's all.'

'I'll leave you to puzzle it out,' said the superintendent. 'In the meantime, I shall go out for a smoke. Let me know when Constable Sharpe returns, though I suspect she will take somewhat longer than required.' And he strolled out, leaving me to wonder whether everyone in my world was determined to behave strangely and talk in riddles.

CHAPTER 10

Steph was back within half an hour, alone. I shot Superintendent Hicks a triumphant look. 'Was the inspector out?'

'No, he was in.' That didn't account for Steph's disappointed face.

'Did you get the chance to talk to him?'

'Briefly. He was about to go into a meeting, but he said he'd pop round in an hour if he could.'

'Did you mention Walton Jail – I mean HMP Liverpool? And Adam?'

'Yes,' said Steph. 'He seemed OK with that.'

'Then why are you fed up?'

'No reason,' said Steph. 'Anyway, I'm not fed up. I'm pleased I managed to get hold of the inspector and he's taking it seriously. Now, if you don't mind, I'm going to the file room. Those files won't process themselves, unfortunately.'

The superintendent and I exchanged glances as she

scurried into the building. 'What's up with her?' I asked.

'I suspect someone wasn't in,' said Superintendent Hicks. 'Or busy.'

'But Inspector Farnsworth *was* in,' I said. 'And while he was busy, he wasn't opposed to our idea and he's coming over. So Steph should be happy.'

Superintendent Hicks tapped the side of his nose. 'The mystery deepens.'

'I do wish you'd stop talking about a mystery. Steph's my friend. If anything was going on, I'd know.'

'Of course you would.' Superintendent Hicks stuck his pipe in his mouth and fumbled for matches.

I left him to it and went up to the detective office. It struck me that we hadn't used it in this case. Everything had taken place either in the file room, in the yard, or at the Athenaeum. I resolved to speak to Steph about that when she was in a better mood. It was a shame not to use all the station's facilities.

There was a knock at the door around fifty minutes later, according to the clock Steph had put on the desk. I ran down and hovered while Steph came up from the basement. Superintendent Hicks strolled in, too.

'I can't stay long,' said Inspector Farnsworth, the minute he was inside. 'I have five minutes before I must be elsewhere.' Despite his words, his eyes were bright and he looked full of pent-up energy. 'There's just enough time to show you what I've found.'

'You found something?' I cried. 'How?'

'I have a subscription to the Ancestry website,' said the inspector. 'I did a few searches last night after work, then checked the British Newspaper Archive, and I found John Finley.' He held up his phone.

'Should we go to the yard?' I asked. 'So that you can get reception?'

He smiled. 'That's very modern of you, Nora. However, as I am old-school, I typed up my findings and printed them out.' He took a folded piece of paper from his inner jacket pocket.

'In that case,' I said, 'shall we go to the detective office?'

'No time.' The inspector unfolded the sheet and spread it against the wall. 'Here he is. John Finley, born the twenty-first of March 1860, son of Thomas and Mary Finley. He's the seventh of ten children, though several didn't live long.'

'Oh no, that's terrible,' said Steph.

'Not unusual in those days,' said Superintendent Hicks. 'Carry on, Farnsworth.'

'Using census records, I tracked him to various addresses. He grew up in Gore Street, Toxteth, and lived there until at least 1871. At the next census, in 1881, he has moved a few streets down to Wesley Street. Among those resident at his address are John

Finley, aged twenty-one, Susan Finley, aged twenty, and three children: John, Susan, and Thomas. Ten years later, in 1891, he, Susan and four children – with different names, I'm afraid – were living in Whitechapel, London. John Finley died in 1894, aged thirty-three. The cause of death is given as internal injuries following assault.'

'Poor man,' I said, and there was a moment's silence.

'Poor man, indeed,' said Superintendent Hicks, looking sceptical. 'You don't know what he's done yet. The assault might have been an act of revenge.'

'Let's not speculate,' said Inspector Farnsworth, and again I was grateful for his calm presence and his ready access to knowledge, even if it did feel like cheating.

'Did you discover any other crimes?' said Steph.

'Mostly, that sort of thing isn't available online,' said Inspector Farnsworth. 'But I went back to the Digital Panopticon site and copied John Finley's record.' He handed another piece of folded paper to Steph. 'Now I really must go.'

'What about visiting Adam? Can we go later today?' She looked like a small child asking for a treat.

'You can go now. I phoned ahead and they're expecting you. Say hello to Adam for me.' He nodded to us, then opened the big front door and left. A minute later, a car started.

'What are we waiting for?' I cried. 'Let's go!'

'Not so fast, Nora,' said Steph. 'I'll have to borrow a police car, unless we're going on the bus. And cover? There's always supposed to be someone on duty at the Bridewell during office hours.'

'That's never bothered you before, Constable Sharpe,' said Superintendent Hicks. 'If you tell the people at Erskine Street that the inspector has sent you to the prison on official business, a car will be no problem.'

'But – but...' Steph looked from me to the superintendent and back, and I recognised an expression I had felt on my own face many times. The expression of someone who was out of her depth.

'Don't worry, Steph,' I said. 'Superintendent Hicks is right. Tell Sergeant Jones what you've been asked to do – visit Walton Jail about a case – and everything will be fine. You'll see.'

Steph sighed out a breath. 'You're right, Nora. It's just— I didn't expect to have to do this alone.'

'You won't be alone,' rumbled Superintendent Hicks. 'We shall be with you. A superintendent and an acting sergeant.' I beamed at him, but I don't think he noticed. 'You're in safe hands.'

'And you know Adam,' I added. 'The inspector's even given you a crib sheet.' I pointed to the paper in her hand.

'Yes,' said Steph, and managed a wavering smile.

As I had predicted, Steph's fears were not realised. She left for the station, and twenty minutes later came back grinning. 'The car's outside.'

I was surprised when Superintendent Hicks sat in the back of the car with me again, but I took it as silent praise for my role in getting Steph to step up. The traffic was light, and we arrived at the prison just after eleven o'clock.

'Right.' Steph put on her hat, checking it in the mirror. 'Let's go.' She set off without opening the door for us. I couldn't decide whether that was because she was focused on the job ahead, or worried that someone would see. Superintendent Hicks and I eased our way through the door and followed her.

Steph walked confidently up to the desk and addressed the prison officer behind the glass. 'Constable Stephanie Sharpe, to visit Mr Fagan. Inspector Farnsworth phoned earlier.'

'Oh yes.' The officer checked a piece of paper. 'Sign in, please, hand over any items on the list, and I'll buzz you through.'

We went into the little lobby between the two doors. Superintendent Hicks frowned as the first door closed. 'It's all right,' I said, 'Adam will fetch us. He works in one of the original buildings. You might remember it.'

'It isn't that,' he said. 'It's—'

At that moment, the other door opened to reveal the elderly prison warder. 'Constable Sharpe,' he said.

'Steph, please,' said Steph.

'Steph it is. And Miss Norris.' His brown eyes crinkled in a smile.

'You can call me Nora, but it's Constable Norris now,' I said, puffing up a little, but he was already looking past me. 'And I believe this is Superintendent Hicks. How do you do, sir.'

'How do you do,' said the superintendent, but he appeared dazed. I wondered whether being shut in the lobby had brought on a funny turn.

'My father used to speak of you,' said Adam. 'He was a warden too, you see. As was my grandfather. All Adam, like myself.'

'Ah!' The superintendent smiled. 'That explains it.'

'We had better not stand here reminiscing,' said Adam. 'Let us consult the ledgers in my sanctum.' And he led us via the same roundabout route to the imposing redbrick building where his office was. I caught the superintendent staring at his neat white ponytail.

'I apologise for the lack of seating,' Adam said, taking up position behind the table in the middle of the room. 'What can I do for you?'

'We're looking for this man,' said Steph, and passed him the sheets of paper. 'John Finley. We want to know whether he was ever a prisoner here. He's currently causing trouble at the Athenaeum.'

'Is he,' said Adam. He stared down his beaky nose at the papers, then reached for a ledger. 'This is volume F of my index, which lists every prisoner who has ever spent time here. There may well be several John Finleys, but the dates are helpful.' He opened the ledger, turned the pages carefully, and ran his bony finger down a column. 'Yes, several John Finleys, of various spellings, and two Jack Finleys. However, both Jacks are too late for this man. We shall try the Johns… Three from the right period. Now for the date of birth…' He tapped the ledger. 'It is this man. He is in the 1883 ledger, page twenty-four, and the 1885 ledger, page fifty. So not much at all.'

'But what of the severity of the crimes?' Superintendent Hicks was leaning forward, ready to pounce, like a cat waiting for a mouse to come out of its hole.

'We shall see, Superintendent.' Adam put the index back and fetched the two ledgers. 'In 1883…' He opened the ledger and riffled through the pages. 'He stole potatoes with an estimated value of fourpence. Sentence: two weeks' imprisonment.'

'Is that it?' exclaimed the superintendent. 'Never mind. Next, please.'

Adam closed the ledger and shelved it. It was all I could do not to hurry him. He opened the second ledger and turned a page. 'This is a little more serious.'

'Go on,' said the superintendent, with a gleam in his eye.

'Pork chops,' said Adam. 'They were more valuable and it was a second offence, so he got a month, but was released early for good behaviour.'

'This makes no sense,' said the superintendent. 'John Finley is supposed to be evil, but from the sound of it, he's stealing to feed his family. Will we ever get to the bottom of this?'

'There is another possibility,' said Adam, and we all looked at him. 'A crime that John Finley was never convicted of.'

'What can we do about that?' asked Steph. 'It's not as if we can go back in time and ask, is it?'

'Not exactly,' said Adam. 'He's at the Athenaeum, you say?'

'That's right,' I replied. 'On the ground floor. Probably because he died before the club was built.'

'That makes sense,' said Adam. 'Very well. I shall ask my line manager for leave of absence.'

'To do what?' asked Superintendent Hicks.

'To visit the Athenaeum with you and summon this John Finley,' Adam replied. 'Perhaps we can find out what he has to say for himself. Let me see… Steph, if you give me your card I can telephone you at Erskine Street station. Or if you don't mind waiting in reception, I could ask n—'

'We'll wait,' said Steph.

Our wait in the prison's reception seemed long, but the clock on the wall told me that it was only a few minutes. It probably felt longer because we couldn't discuss the case. 'Are you all right now?' I asked the superintendent.

'Yes, fine,' he replied, folding his arms. But he was still frowning.

'Did it bring back memories?'

'In a manner of speaking. Not that I was here often.'

'Oh,' I said, and left it at that.

Eventually, Adam reappeared. 'My line manager says I may take an early lunch. Steph, could you telephone the Athenaeum and let them know we are on our way?'

'Of course,' said Steph.

'Then I shall get changed. I doubt the club will welcome someone in a prison officer's uniform. I shall meet you outside in a few minutes.' He executed a half bow and left.

I clapped my hands together. 'Things are finally moving!'

'Mmm,' said Superintendent Hicks.

Steph stood up. 'I'll head outside.' She signed herself out at the desk and reclaimed her phone.

'What's up?' I asked Superintendent Hicks, as we

stood by the prison entrance. Steph had moved away to phone the Athenaeum.

'I know that man,' he said. 'I'd swear to it.'

'Don't be silly. You, er, moved on in the sixties. I don't know how old Adam is, but even if he's in his seventies, he'd have been in his teens then. Maybe you knew his dad or his grandad.'

'It wasn't in the sixties,' said Superintendent Hicks. 'I was too senior to mess around in prisons by then.'

Too old, I thought. 'So when was it?'

'I started in 1911. Never had much to do with the prison in those days, but later, I'd visit prisoners there or attend a meeting. I remember Fagan. He was on the in-and-out desk and he wrote everyone down in a big ledger. I remember his bony hand moving across the page. He looked a bit younger than the man we've met, but not much. And he was the spit of him.'

'That's probably a strong family resemblance,' I said.

'It isn't only that,' said Superintendent Hicks. 'I spent so long staring at Mr Fagan's hand over the years that I knew it nearly as well as my own. There was a small mole at the base of the thumb, and a brown age spot the shape of Australia. The man we just met has got them, too.'

CHAPTER 11

'Adam can't be the person you knew,' I said. 'He just can't.'

'And there's no such thing as ghosts, I suppose?' said Superintendent Hicks.

'What you're suggesting is impossible. It has to be.' My head was spinning. I felt the urge to grab something, and knowing I couldn't made it worse.

'Clearly it isn't,' he said, drily. 'What I want to know is—'

'All sorted,' called Steph, and joined us. 'I've spoken to Jude and he's fine with us coming over. I haven't said exactly what we're doing, obviously. Just that we're bringing a colleague who has a great deal of experience with ghosts.'

'Indeed he does,' said Superintendent Hicks, and I shot him a look. 'Speak of the devil, here he comes.'

Adam, now dressed in a dark suit, a white shirt, and a knitted tie, walked towards us.

'See those lapels?' said the superintendent. 'I used to have a suit like that.'

'So he has good taste in clothes,' I said, but my heart wasn't in it. Steph walked to meet him, but I couldn't follow her. I didn't know what to do.

'Probably best to travel separately,' Adam said, as he approached with Steph. 'I'll have to come straight back, and I'm sure you have other business to attend to.'

Thank heavens, I thought. *At least I won't have to travel in a car with him.*

Superintendent Hicks was studying Adam, his mouth set in a firm line. 'You didn't mean that, did you?' I whispered. 'About the devil.'

'It's just an expression, Nora,' he murmured. 'To be perfectly honest, I'm not sure what I think. He's solid enough, but there's something about him. And he can see us, of course. What I do know is that we'd better not inform Constable Sharpe until after we've finished at the Athenaeum. I don't want her to overreact to – whatever he is.'

'Will you say anything to Adam?'

He shrugged.

Steph and Adam parted, Steph making for the police car. She mouthed something to us which looked like *Are you coming, or what?*

'We have been summoned,' said Superintendent Hicks, and strolled towards her.

As we drove into the city centre, my mind was all over the place. Adam wasn't a ghost. He couldn't be a ghost, because everyone could see him and he could handle everyday things such as a pen and a door pass. And he wasn't transparent in the slightest. So presumably he was alive. Could the superintendent be mistaken? But then I remembered Adam's job as the prison's unofficial historian – how convenient – and what he'd said to the superintendent about his father and grandfather, both with the same name and occupying the same job at the same prison. That was definitely suspicious. But how could I find out more about Adam, and what would I do if I did? Adam was a good person who was helping us. At least, I hoped so.

We stopped at a red light. 'Are you all right back there?' asked Steph. 'You're very quiet.'

'Just thinking over the case,' I replied.

'Well, hopefully it's drawing to a close,' said Steph. 'Adam will summon John Finley and we'll have a chat. Then we can deal with the matter, tie up the loose ends and find a proper case to work on. Something we can get our teeth into.' The light turned green and the car moved off smoothly.

Steph parked in what I was coming to think of as our usual place by the Old Post Office pub. 'I've told Adam where we'll be,' she said. 'We'll wait for him and go in together.'

Fairly soon afterwards, a boxy brown car pulled up behind us.

'A Hillman Imp, as I live and breathe,' said Superintendent Hicks. 'Or don't.' He stared at the car. 'So what will this Adam Fagan do, exactly? You've mentioned summoning a couple of times, Constable Sharpe.'

'Oh yes, I forgot you wouldn't know,' said Steph. 'During our last case, Adam summoned two suspects to the prison, in the form of their ghosts. Both confessed, and they were taken to judgement.'

'Were they,' said the superintendent, not sounding particularly impressed. 'So he's got special powers, this Adam.'

'He has, yes,' said Steph.

'I wonder what else he can do.' He stared out of the back window as Adam approached.

We got out and walked down the street towards the Athenaeum. 'As I am your guest, Steph, I shall put myself in your hands,' said Adam. 'Just let me know what you want me to do and when, and I shall do my best.'

The superintendent raised his eyebrows at me and I looked away.

Perhaps I was mistaken or it was a trick of the light, but Jude seemed to roll his eyes when he saw us. 'Good afternoon,' he said. 'I'm afraid I won't be able to accompany you today, as we are particularly busy around lunchtime.' As if to illustrate this, a small group of people began walking upstairs.

'That's fine, Jude,' said Steph. She gestured to Adam. 'This is Mr Fagan, who I mentioned on the phone.'

'Oh yes.' Jude offered a hand and Adam shook it firmly. I raised my eyebrows at the superintendent, who harrumphed. 'Pleased to meet you, Mr Fagan. Do come this way. I'll have to ask you both to sign in.'

'Of course,' said Adam, and we walked inside. 'Lovely place,' he commented, looking about him. 'I'm surprised I haven't managed to visit before.'

'So am I,' said Superintendent Hicks, and I glared at him.

A phone rang in Jude's cubbyhole and he glanced at the door. 'As I said, very busy. Would you mind terribly if I left you to get on?' And without waiting for an answer, he hastened to his room.

'Where is the best place to try, Adam?' asked Steph.

Adam considered. 'It should work anywhere. Where will cause the least disruption?'

'Most of the rooms the club members use are upstairs,' I said. 'As long as we aren't in the entrance hall, and out of view of the staircase, it should be fine.'

'What she said,' said Steph. She seemed much

happier since teaming up with Adam. I suppose it was nice for her to have a visible colleague once more. 'Let's find somewhere quiet.'

We passed through the entrance hall and found a small, empty cloakroom. 'This will do,' said Adam. 'I'd rather we were as far from the public gaze as possible. Especially if this spirit is . . . let's say undisciplined.'

I was already some distance from Adam, but I retreated until I was standing in the doorway.

'Yes, it may be a good idea to stand back,' said Adam, and Steph and the superintendent joined me.

'Time to work your magic, Mr Fagan,' said the superintendent. 'Bring on the show.'

Adam gave him a long look. 'It isn't a show, Superintendent, and it's hardly a joking matter.'

'I do beg your pardon,' said Superintendent Hicks, not sounding sorry at all.

Adam took a few deep breaths and raised his right hand. 'John Finley, you are wanted for questioning. Show yourself!'

And nothing happened. I tried to remember how it had worked the last time, in Walton Jail. Had Bill Cracknell appeared out of nowhere, or faded into view?

Adam looked at his hand, then raised it again. 'John Finley, I summon you!'

The silence was deafening.

'Maybe he prefers Jack,' said Steph. 'That was mentioned as an alias.'

'Let's try it, then. Jack Finley, I summon you. Show yourself!'

No response.

'John Finley, also known as Jack Finley, you are wanted for questioning!'

'There must be an awful lot of John or Jack Finleys out there,' I said. 'Maybe it isn't clear which one you mean.'

Adam took the paper Inspector Farnsworth had given us from his suit pocket. 'John Finley, also known as Jack Finley, born on the twenty-first of March 1860, formerly of Gore Street and Wesley Street in Liverpool, I hereby summon you to appear.' But it was more a question than a command.

Steph was frowning. 'Why isn't it working?'

'I don't know,' said Adam. 'To be honest, it isn't an exact science. And I've never done this outside HMP Liverpool. Perhaps I have no authority to summon unless I am within the prison boundary.'

'Or maybe it's something to do with John Finley himself,' said Superintendent Hicks. 'A slippery customer all round.' He seemed much more cheerful now that Adam had failed.

'Maybe it isn't that,' I said. 'Perhaps, because John Finley didn't do anything very bad and he served his sentence, there was no reason for him to answer your summons.'

'All these are possible,' said Adam. 'But the fact remains that I cannot summon John Finley today. I do apologise for the wasted trip, Steph.'

'It's not your fault,' said Steph, though she looked positively woebegone.

'Is it worth speaking to Reverend Bell?' asked the superintendent. 'Not that he'll know anything.'

Steph made a face. 'At the moment, he's nice and quiet. If he finds out we tried something today and failed, he might kick off again.'

'Oh, so he's the one causing a commotion?' said Adam. 'I hadn't realised.'

'I'm sorry, I thought I'd explained.' Steph pinched the bridge of her nose. 'It's just that it's been rather a day.' For a moment, none of us knew what to say.

Adam shifted from foot to foot. 'I'm truly sorry I couldn't help. I'd better get back to work. Do let me know if there's anything further I can do for you.' He nodded to us, then walked towards the entrance hall with long, measured strides, his ponytail bobbing as he went.

Superintendent Hicks turned to Steph. 'What now, Constable Sharpe?'

'I have no idea,' Steph replied, shaking her head. 'I have absolutely no idea.'

CHAPTER 12

Steph sat down on the cloakroom bench and ran her fingers through her short dark hair. 'What can we do?'

Superintendent Hicks nudged me, then walked to the other end of the cloakroom. 'Should we tell her?' he murmured.

'Tell her what?'

He directed a steely gaze at the door which Adam had gone through less than a minute ago. 'You know what.'

'No. Absolutely not. It won't solve anything. In fact, all it will do is distract everyone from what we're meant to be doing. Which is solving this.'

'What are you two muttering about?' Steph looked at me suspiciously. 'What's going on?'

'Nothing,' I said. 'Just trying to work out what to do. We seem to be setting about this the wrong way.'

Steph shrugged. 'Got any better ideas?'

I walked over and sat on the bench beside her. 'Not

at the moment, but I'm working on it. Let's set out what we know.'

'That won't take long.' But Steph looked a tiny bit brighter.

I beckoned to the superintendent. 'Come and help. We need all the brains we can get.'

'I'll take that as a compliment,' said Superintendent Hicks, and came to join us.

'John Finley,' I said. 'We know a little about him, and that's much more than most people. The Rev didn't even know his name. So how does he know he's evil?'

'He's stolen things,' said Steph. 'Could that be what he's doing here? Can ghosts steal things?'

'Not usually,' said Superintendent Hicks. He stood up and grasped at one of the metal pegs, but his fingers went through it.

'But it must be possible,' said Steph. 'Poltergeists?'

'Yes,' I replied. 'That's why we're here, because the Rev can move things. Or at least, he can create a draught which moves things. And we can smell him.'

'Can't we just,' muttered Superintendent Hicks.

'What if this John Finley is more powerful?' I stood up and paced, taken with my own idea. 'Maybe it isn't so much what he's done, but Reverend Bell knows Finley's more powerful than him, and he's scared.'

'What is he scared of, exactly?' said Superintendent Hicks. 'I mean, it's not as if this Finley could do anything to him. Even if he could, he can't come upstairs. He's stuck on the ground floor. So all the Rev would have to do is stay on the upper levels of the club.'

'But he wouldn't want to,' I replied. 'From what I've seen of Reverend Bell, he's a snob. So maybe it's partly that he's scared and partly that he's resentful. And maybe John Finley *has* been stealing things, or at least moving them.'

Steph frowned. 'Did you feel that?'

'No, what?'

'That breeze.'

Superintendent Hicks surveyed the room, then pointed to an air vent near the ceiling. 'It was probably that, Constable Sharpe.'

'That, or something else,' I said. 'Or should I say *someone* else.'

Steph jumped to her feet. 'Right, let's move.'

'Are we leaving?' I asked.

'Not yet.' Steph was breathing rapidly and there was a dangerous glint in her eye. 'I can't believe we've been discussing the case where John Finley can hear us. But at least we can ask whether anything has gone missing lately. Perhaps that's what the Rev is sensing.'

'It's worth a try,' said Superintendent Hicks. 'I suppose anything is worth a try.'

Steph marched out of the cloakroom and we followed her to Jude's cubbyhole. However, Jude wasn't there. In his place was a shorter, stockier man with thinning, sandy hair. 'Can I help— Oh, good afternoon, officer. I hope nothing is amiss.'

'Just a routine check,' said Steph. 'Has Jude finished for the day?'

'He's having his lunch. I'm filling in for him, so I'm afraid I can't help. He'll be' – he checked his watch – 'about half an hour. One of his friends who is a member is in today, so Jude is taking the opportunity to catch up.'

'Marvellous,' said Steph. 'I literally have one question for him, so I'm sure he won't mind. He'll be in the dining room?'

'Yes, but I don't—'

'Thank you so much.' And Steph was climbing the stairs before the man had a chance to close his mouth.

'Are you sure this is a good idea, Steph?' I asked.

'It's the best we've got,' said Steph, increasing her pace. 'I don't want Inspector Farnsworth to think we've wasted our time. We have to make the most of this opportunity.'

'There's making the most of the opportunity, Constable Sharpe, and then there's—'

'I'm not arguing with you, Superintendent,' said Steph. 'I'm saving my breath for the stairs.' By the time we reached the dining room at the top of the building she was rather pink.

'I'm sure the inspector will understand, Steph,' I said. 'This sort of work is bound to be uncertain.'

'I prefer as little uncertainty as possible,' said Steph, and walked into the dining room. The superintendent and I exchanged glances, and followed.

The room was perhaps a third full. *So much for Jude saying how busy it was*, I thought, then reflected that several of the club members might well have dined and left to read the papers or have a little snooze in an armchair. Certainly, the delicious aromas suggested that several people had had a nice lunch that day. For a moment, I recalled the feeling of getting home after a hard shift, kicking off my work shoes and putting my feet on the fender to warm before Ma told me off. But Steph was making her way across the room, and the buzz of conversation had decreased considerably.

Jude was sitting near the back of the room, opposite a young man in a navy jacket, and he was currently frozen, a forkful of meat pie halfway to his mouth. He set it down hastily. 'Constable Sharpe, is something the matter?'

'No, not at all,' said Steph. She crouched to bring herself to Jude's eye level. 'I'm sorry to disturb you during your lunch. I have a question for you.'

Jude's gaze was shifting between Steph and the

room in general. 'I, er... We should probably go outside, if this is related to the investigation.'

'It won't take a moment,' said Steph. 'I wondered if you could tell me whether anything has gone missing recently.'

Jude's eyes widened. 'Gone missing?'

'Yes. Money, or personal items, or—'

Something whooshed by, and in its wake was a sickening floral smell. 'Oh no!' I cried. 'The Rev is here!'

'What?' Steph stood up and looked around the room.

A man in a striped tie exclaimed as his wine glass tipped over. 'What's going on?' cried his companion.

At another table, a woman struggled to her feet as the tablecloth and everything on it began to move.

'Calm down!' shouted Steph. I wasn't sure if she was addressing the Rev or all the club's members. 'Everyone stay calm!'

A fork rose slowly into the air, then flew across the room, landing on the carpet. I heard a mocking laugh, and saw a Rev-shaped haze among the tables. 'He's there!' I cried, pointing.

A portly grey-haired man in a suit stood up and surveyed the room. Steph gasped and backed towards the door. 'This nonsense must cease immediately!' he declared. He looked familiar, and I wondered where I had seen him before.

Everyone stopped moving. A menu fell over.

'Constable Sharpe!' he barked, and Steph stopped dead. 'A word, if you would.'

'But I—'

'Now!' He strode out of the dining room and Steph scurried after him.

I wasn't sure whether to follow, but Superintendent Hicks hurried past me, and I figured that if he was going to listen in then I might as well. 'Perhaps we can support her,' I said.

'We did try to stop her,' said the superintendent.

The door slammed as we approached it, but we went through it anyway, emerging in a tense silence.

'You must have something to say for yourself,' the man said, in an undertone which was far more frightening than if he had bellowed.

'It was just—'

'I don't want to hear it! In fact, what I do want to know is why you are here on your own. Inspector Farnsworth ought to know better than that.'

'I'm not on my own,' Steph murmured.

'Oh, really?' The man made an exaggerated show of looking about him. 'I didn't see any of your colleagues in there, unless they were hiding under the tables.'

Steph bit her lip, and was silent.

'When I told Inspector Farnsworth to sort out this business at the Athenaeum, I did *not* expect one of his team to enter my club at one of its busiest times and cause a sensation in my presence!'

'We were trying to—'

'I don't care what you were trying to do. What you *did* is scare an awful lot of people, some of whom are friends of mine. Now, I have no idea what went on in there, but if anything like that happens again – well, I'm not sure there will be a place for you in Merseyside Police.' He scowled at Steph. 'There's no point in crying, Constable Sharpe.'

'I'm not crying, Chief Inspector,' Steph said, in a wobbly voice. *So this is the Chief they all talk about*, I thought.

He continued to stare at her, and the scowl faded a little. 'I'm going back to finish my lunch,' he said, 'assuming it isn't on the floor. By the time I finish, Constable Sharpe, I expect you to be gone. And I don't want to see you for a very long time.' He wrenched open the dining-room door, stepped through, and glared at Steph as he shut it smartly behind him.

CHAPTER 13

Steph stared at the closed door for a moment, then set off downstairs.

'Are you all right, Steph?' I asked, but she didn't reply. If anything, she moved faster, changing sides as she met people coming up. I wanted to apologise for their startled looks.

'Best leave her alone for a bit,' muttered Superintendent Hicks. 'I imagine that stung.'

'Stung? Huh,' Steph said, darkly. 'What you just saw was probably the end of my career. I'll be stuck at a desk for ever. I'll probably spend the next ten years of my life rubber-stamping files at the Bridewell, with only you two for company.'

'Well,' I said, 'we'll be glad to have you. You're an excellent policewoman, Steph.'

'Officer, Nora,' she snapped. 'Police officer. How many times have I told you?'

I was about to make a smart reply when

Superintendent Hicks caught my eye and shook his head.

I seethed quietly all the way to the ground floor. Steph made straight for the front door.

'Excuse me!' The substitute concierge stuck his head out of the cubbyhole. 'Did you sign in?'

'Yes, we did,' Steph replied.

He frowned. 'We?'

Steph was silent for a moment. 'I came with a Mr Fagan. He's already left.'

'Oh, I see.' He chuckled. 'For a moment, I thought you meant the Royal we.'

'Not on this occasion,' said Steph, and scrawled the time next to her name.

'The chief inspector will probably have forgotten it by the time he's finished his lunch,' I said, as we hurried down the street.

Steph glared at me. 'Can we talk about something else? In fact, can you not talk at all. I need to concentrate on driving and as you'll understand, I have a lot on my mind.'

The journey back was silent except for the car radio, which Steph had turned up. At one point I asked if it had got stuck, but Steph told me that was how drum and bass music was meant to sound. After that, I kept quiet.

I was glad when Steph came to an abrupt stop outside the Bridewell. The journey had not been smooth, with growls from the car's engine, last-minute stops, and corners taken far too fast, in my opinion. 'There you go,' she said. 'I'm taking the car to Erskine Street. I'll walk back.'

'See you soon, Steph. I hope the walk does you good.'

Steph snorted. 'Please get out, Nora.'

We did as we were told and watched the car roar away. I wondered if Steph had seen another one of those Fast and Furious films lately. I hoped not. They might be a bad influence.

'Oh dear,' I said, as Superintendent Hicks and I passed through the gates to the yard. Queen Vic and Prince were standing there like a welcoming committee. 'I do hope Steph cheers up.'

'Maybe it will blow over,' said the superintendent, pulling out his pipe. 'The Chief will talk to Farnsworth, who'll explain things. He's that sort of chap.'

I leaned my forehead on Queen Vic's flank. 'I hope you're right. Steph was doing her best, even if it wasn't the right thing on this occasion. She has a lot of potential.'

'Spoken like someone with a hundred years of hindsight,' the superintendent replied.

I looked round at him. 'What do you mean?'

'You'd have done exactly the same thing at her age. In with both feet and all guns blazing.'

I reflected on this. 'Yes, I probably would. I was desperate to make my mark and become a real police officer.' I met his eyes. 'What about you?'

Superintendent Hicks searched his pockets and brought out his tobacco pouch. 'I'd certainly have considered it, but with one important addition.'

'Which is?'

'I'd have checked who was in the room first. Given how many people were there, I would definitely have thought twice.'

'Easy to be wise after the event,' I said.

'Isn't it.'

We stayed there, me stroking Queen Vic's mane and the superintendent sitting and smoking on the metal stairs, until we heard a loud slam.

'Wonder who that is,' said Superintendent Hicks, and got to his feet.

We roamed the station in search of Steph, and eventually found her not in the file room, nor the detective office, but sitting in one of the cells, all bunched up. 'You were quick,' I commented.

Steph looked up at me. 'I was hardly going to hang around, was I? Not after that.'

'Was Inspector Farnsworth really cross?' I asked.

'Worse than that. He was on the phone.'

'Ah,' said the superintendent.

'The Chief was probably giving him the hairdryer treatment,' said Steph, 'and he'll pass it on to me.'

'I doubt it,' I said, though I had no idea what the hairdryer treatment might be. 'Inspector Farnsworth's too nice to do that.'

'We'll see,' said Steph, and put her chin on her knees.

Superintendent Hicks and I stood and fidgeted. It didn't seem right to leave Steph alone, but there wasn't a great deal we could do. I wished there had been a clock in the cell, since I had no idea how long we might be stuck there. Presumably until Steph went home, or until Inspector Farnsworth did whatever he was going to do...

'Hello?' The voice sounded like Tasha's. 'Steph, are you there?'

For the first time, I was actually pleased that Tasha had called round to the Bridewell. She and Steph were very good friends. Perhaps she could cheer Steph up.

'Steph, where are you? I know you're here: you told Huw you were going to the Bridewell when you gave him the keys. Come out, come out, wherever you are!' She giggled.

Slowly, Steph got to her feet. 'I'm coming,' she called, and left without so much as a glance at us.

'Typical,' I said, sourly. 'That Tasha comes round and off she goes. Not even a thank you to the people who've tried to lift her spirits.'

'The spirits who lift spirits,' said Superintendent Hicks. 'That's rather good.'

'It wasn't intentional,' I said, and left the cell.

Steph and Tasha were standing by the stairs which led up to the detective office. 'Where have you been?' asked Tasha. 'Sam said you were looking for me this morning, and she said I'd missed you again just now. I was in the loo.'

'Uh-huh,' said Steph. 'So have you come round to find out what I was up to?'

Tasha grinned. 'Not precisely. I mean, obviously I'm curious as to why you borrowed a police car and where you went. However, on this occasion I come bearing a message from Inspector Farnsworth.' Steph gasped, but Tasha didn't notice. 'He said he'd like a word.'

'Oh God,' muttered Steph.

'What's up?' Tasha put a hand on Steph's arm. 'You've gone white as a sheet. I didn't think people actually did that.'

'I'm fine,' said Steph, looking anything but. 'Does he want me to go round there?'

'No, he'll come over. I was passing his office when he put the phone down and called me. He said he had a couple of things to attend to, but then he'd come and see you.'

'Right,' Steph croaked, and ran her finger around the inside of her collar.

'It's probably nothing,' said Tasha. 'I bet he fancies a change of scene. He's been in meetings all day.'

'How did he seem?' asked Steph, with an expression which suggested she expected an instant death sentence.

Tasha's brow furrowed. 'It's hard to describe. A bit troubled, and also a bit…' She screwed up her mouth as she thought, making herself look completely ridiculous. 'As if he was heading for the edge of a cliff and he'd only just seen in time.'

'Ohhh…' Steph moved to the banister and clutched it.

Tasha laughed. 'I'm sure it's not that bad! Probably indigestion.'

'Or the hairdryer treatment,' said Superintendent Hicks.

'Shut up!' cried Steph, glaring at us. 'You're not helping.'

Tasha drew back as if Steph had slapped her. 'You asked me! I was trying to describe it, that's all.'

'I didn't mean you,' said Steph, who was clinging to the wrought-iron banister as if she had been shipwrecked. Come to think of it, she did look rather seasick.

Tasha frowned. 'Then who did you mean?' The frown deepened. 'The inspector did know you were borrowing a car, didn't he?'

'Yes! Well, not directly, but he knew where I was going and that I'd need a car.'

'So where were you going?'

Steph said nothing.

'You'll probably feel better if you tell her, Steph,' I said. 'Secrets never help.'

'I'm not sure I can tell you,' said Steph, looking everywhere but at Tasha.

'Why not? Is it top secret?' Tasha laughed, but it faded quickly. 'What are you so scared of, Steph? Have you done something wrong?'

'Not exactly,' Steph murmured.

'Tell her the truth!' I cried. 'She's your friend. She'll understand.'

'She won't,' Steph said darkly.

'I'm right here,' said Tasha, 'in case you've forgotten.'

'It's only fair that you tell her,' said Superintendent Hicks. 'How can you have any sort of relationship without trust?'

'Exactly,' I chimed in. 'Friends trust one another.'

'What are you looking at?' said Tasha. 'What's going on? Are you ill?'

'I sometimes wonder,' said Steph. 'All that reassures me is that Inspector Farnsworth can see them too. We're not alone, Tasha.' She waved a hand at us. 'You can't see them, but standing over there are Nora Norris and Superintendent Hicks. They're police officers who also happen to be ghosts.'

'*What?*'

'They were out with me today, at HMP Liverpool

and the Athenaeum Club, investigating a disturbance involving a couple of other ghosts.'

'Is that the best you can do?' There was a gleam in Tasha's eye, and the corner of her mouth curved up in a smile that wasn't.

Steph sighed, and all the air seemed to go out of her. 'It's the truth, Tasha. I'm sorry.'

'So am I,' said Tasha. 'If you wanted to finish with me – not that we'd really started – you could have invented a sick relative you had to visit, or something. There's no need to convince me that you're actually insane.'

'I'm not!' cried Steph. 'There are ghosts here, I swear it! And it's because of a ghost that I'm facing the sack.'

Tasha stared at her. The smirk had gone, and in its place was a look of deepest contempt. 'I don't understand you, Steph. When we first met, I thought you were a bit obsessed with work, maybe, but nice, dependable… Other things, too… But this is off the scale. I don't know if you're working on some secret project while the rest of us handle the day-to-day stuff, but whatever it is, it's obviously gone to your head. So much so that you spin a stack of lies to someone who – who… Oh, forget it. I've delivered your message, and I'm done. Goodbye, Steph.'

Tasha turned with a swish of her auburn hair, flung open the door, and slammed it behind her. Very faintly, I heard the word 'Ghosts!', said with utter loathing.

'And I thought the day couldn't get worse,' said Steph. She let go of the banister and sank into a sad little heap on the floor.

CHAPTER 14

Superintendent Hicks and I stared miserably at each other, not sure what to do. Mere words didn't seem enough, and besides, I was worried about saying the wrong thing. A hand on the arm or a gentle hug felt right, but that was impossible.

'Um . . . what would help?' I asked.

Steph raised her head. 'I don't know. Maybe nothing can help.'

'I'm so sorry,' said Superintendent Hicks.

There was a long silence. 'It wasn't your fault,' Steph said, at last. 'You two can't help being ghosts. I can't help seeing and speaking to you, and it isn't Tasha's fault that she doesn't know you're there.'

'I'm still sorry,' said the superintendent, and the sincerity in his tone surprised me. It wasn't that I didn't think him capable of being sincere, but I had grown so used to him being a gruff, irascible old man that I had forgotten he might have feelings. Indeed, I was beginning to wonder what else I had missed.

'Thank you,' said Steph, and continued to stare at the opposite wall.

A few minutes later, a knock sounded at the front door. 'May I come in?' said Inspector Farnsworth. His voice was much as usual, though a shade more careful.

'Why not,' said Steph. 'What more do I have to lose?' she muttered. She got up and opened the door. 'I'm sorry about— Oh!'

'I met Constable Saunders and she told me a little of what happened.' The inspector walked in, followed by Tasha. Her expression was neutral, but her face was flushed. I wondered what she was thinking. 'I thought it might be a good idea to clear the air.'

Steph glanced at Tasha, then away again.

Inspector Farnsworth turned to Tasha. 'Constable Saunders, from what you've told me, Constable Sharpe inadvertently revealed something about the Bridewell.'

Tasha nodded, her expression unchanged.

'I shall ask you to keep what follows to yourself for the time being. Do you understand?'

Another nod.

'Constable Sharpe – Steph – isn't the only person who can see and speak with the ghosts who reside at the Bridewell. I have known Nora Norris for a few months, and recently became acquainted with

Superintendent Hicks.'

Superintendent Hicks executed a sort of half bow, while a strange noise came out of Tasha. Her eyes were bulging slightly.

'I realise this must be difficult to comprehend, but what can we do to convince you we are telling the truth?'

'I don't know,' said Tasha, gazing around as if she might be surrounded by invisible people.

'Can you tell her where we're standing?' I said. 'That could help.'

'Good idea, Nora,' said the inspector, and Tasha's eyes opened even wider. 'Constable Saunders, Nora and the superintendent are standing together, about four feet from Constable Sharpe, on her right-hand side. No other ghosts are present.'

'None that we know of, anyway,' said Steph. 'Sorry. That probably complicates things.'

'All right,' said Tasha, 'I'll play along. Convince me there are ghosts in this room.'

'Hmm.' The inspector thought. 'That may be difficult.' He turned to us. 'I don't suppose either of you two could move something?'

'We're not the Rev,' said Superintendent Hicks. 'We don't do that sort of thing.'

'I have an idea,' I said slowly. 'Steph, is the *Observer Magazine* still downstairs in the file room?'

'Probably,' said Steph. 'Although I don't think now

is the time for a read.'

'On the contrary,' I said. 'It could help us show Tasha that we're really here.'

Tasha looked from Steph to the inspector. 'I'm starting to wonder what the pair of you get out of this.'

'Exactly,' said Inspector Farnsworth. 'There's no sensible reason to do it, unless it's true. Steph, would you mind fetching the magazine Nora mentioned and giving it to Tasha?'

Steph scrambled to her feet. 'Back in a couple of minutes,' she said, pulling out her ring of keys. But she spoke not to Inspector Farnsworth but Tasha, who was staring at her with an unreadable expression.

The silence while we waited for Steph was extremely uncomfortable. Tasha stared at the floor as if challenging it to start something, with occasional glares around the hallway. The inspector, meanwhile, got out his phone and stroked the screen with his forefinger, which apparently meant he was reading. Luckily, Steph was back quickly. She handed the magazine to Tasha without a word.

'Right,' said Inspector Farnsworth, putting his phone away. 'Nora, what's your idea?'

'I thought you two could stand facing Tasha and she could ask you what was on the page of the magazine she was reading.'

'I get it.' Steph joined the inspector on the other

side of the corridor. 'Tasha, could you find the recipe section and ask us about it?'

Tasha gave Steph a long look which suggested she'd never heard anything so ridiculous in her life. 'Fine.' She opened the magazine, peered at it, then riffled through the pages. She found a page and studied it for some time. 'On page fifty-nine, what's the fifth ingredient in the first recipe?'

I walked to Tasha and read over her shoulder. 'Double cream.'

'Double cream,' said Steph.

Tasha gave Steph a hard stare. 'You could have guessed that. How much double cream?'

'Seventy-five—' I stopped. 'It says ML. What's an ML?'

'It means millilitres, Nora,' said Steph. 'Seventy-five millilitres.'

'What's wrong with fluid ounces? Or pints?'

'The world has moved on, Nora,' said Inspector Farnsworth. 'Not always for the better.'

'For all I know, this is a memory trick,' said Tasha.

'Then I'll answer the next question,' said the inspector. 'I certainly don't have enough spare brain capacity to memorise a whole magazine.'

'In that case, move away from each other.' Tasha busied herself with the magazine again. 'Who made the dress that Claudia Winkleman is wearing on page twenty-four?'

'Zadig and Voltaire,' I said. 'Although I'm not sure I'm pronouncing it right.'

'Zadig and Voltaire,' said Inspector Farnsworth. 'And I don't know how to say it either.'

'It is a lovely dress,' I said. 'Though it's a shame she didn't get her hair cut before they took the photos. Her fringe is right in her eyes.'

'What are you thinking, Tasha?' Steph asked quietly.

'You're doing something,' said Tasha. She opened the magazine to another page. 'What's the third word on the third line of page eighty-three?'

'Fashionista,' I said, and the inspector relayed it. 'What sort of word is that?'

'As I said, Nora, things don't always improve for the better, and that includes the English language.'

'The last word on the same page.'

'Stockists,' I replied.

'Stockists,' Steph and the inspector said, together.

Tasha closed and reopened the magazine. Her knuckles were white. 'The second word in the note from the editor.'

'My.'

'My,' they chorused.

Tasha flung the magazine at the wall. 'They're not real. This can't be real! Ghosts don't exist. You can't just bring me here and expect me to – to change my mind!' She was trembling, and her eyes shone with tears.

Steph went to her. 'I felt pretty much the same when I first saw Nora,' she said. 'But she's a young woman like us, only – well, a hundred years in the past. Don't be scared of her. Or the superintendent. He's just grumpy.' She reached towards Tasha.

Tasha pulled back as if Steph's hand would burn her. 'Don't touch me!' she shouted. 'Leave me alone, Steph!' She cast a hunted look around her, then bolted upstairs.

Above us, a door slammed.

Inspector Farnsworth crossed the room and patted Steph on the shoulder. 'I'd give her five minutes, Steph. Maybe ten.'

Steph was gazing upwards, in the rough direction of the detective office. 'Do you think she'll forgive me?'

'What for?' I asked.

'For turning her world upside down.' She said the words simply, like a child.

'I'm sure she will,' said Superintendent Hicks. 'She needs time to get used to the idea. If Tasha wants to be with you, she'll find a way to make sense of it.'

And there it was: the thing that had been left unsaid. The mystery Superintendent Hicks had teased me about. Everything clicked into place. 'So you and Tasha are . . . courting? Walking out together?'

'Yes,' said Steph. 'Well, we were.'

And just like that, my world did a little flip. I was thinking that would never have happened in my day when I remembered my older sister Elsie, who had moved out of home to share rooms with her great friend, Rita. Whenever Elsie came round after that, Ma always asked whether she had found herself a nice young man yet, but Elsie shook her brown curls at Ma and laughed. Then there were the two middle-aged ladies with bobbed hair who I often saw at weekends, sitting on a bench together at Kensington Gardens, hands touching. *In your own way, Nora, you were as blind as Tasha. No, more so: it was in front of you the whole time, and you missed it.*

'Steph?' Tasha croaked overhead.

Steph practically sprang to attention. 'Yes?'

'Can you come up?' A pause. 'Please?'

'I'm coming!' called Steph, and raced upstairs so fast that I was surprised she didn't fall over her own feet.

Inspector Farnsworth watched her go, then closed his eyes and let out a slow breath. 'I think they'll be all right.'

'What do we do?' I asked. 'Do we wait? Do we go away and leave them?'

'I have a better idea,' said Inspector Farnsworth. 'You can fill me in on what's happened today. I've had the Chief's version' – he grimaced – 'but I suspect there was more to it than that.'

'What a good idea,' I said, and plunged in, relieved to have something less earth-shattering to think about.

I was just at the part where the Chief was telling Steph off when the door creaked upstairs. 'Shh,' said the superintendent.

We waited. There were slow footsteps, then Steph and Tasha appeared on the landing. Tasha's long auburn hair could have done with a brush, and her eye make-up was smudged. Even Steph's short hair was untidy. However, they were both smiling, though those smiles weren't quite steady. They came downstairs side by side, holding hands.

Tasha didn't seem to know where to look. 'I'm sorry I can't see you or hear you,' she said, gazing at the wall, 'but I accept that you're there.'

'It's a start,' said Superintendent Hicks.

Tasha's eyebrows shot up. 'Did one of them speak?'

Steph grinned. 'You're getting there.' She ruffled Tasha's hair. I thought Tasha might be offended, but she didn't mind at all.

CHAPTER 15

'Now we're all together,' said Inspector Farnsworth, studiously not looking at anyone in particular, 'I should tell you my original reason for dropping in. The Chief rang me earlier, and it's fair to say that he isn't best pleased.'

Steph grimaced, and Tasha squeezed her hand.

'Steph, I'm not suggesting you did the wrong thing, because I don't know what I would have done in the circumstances. However, it had an unfortunate effect.'

'It certainly did,' said Superintendent Hicks.

'The result of which,' Inspector Farnsworth continued, 'is that the Chief says if we don't, and I quote, "get rid of whatever it is at the Athenaeum toot sweet", he will arrange an exorcism himself.'

I winced. 'Then we'll never get to the bottom of the case.'

'Precisely,' said the inspector. 'So time is of the

essence. But the Rev's reaction may give us a clue. Steph, what did you say before the Rev caused the disturbance?'

Steph thought. 'I was talking to Jude. I asked him whether any money or personal items had gone missing and then the Rev kicked off.'

'Hmm,' said Inspector Farnsworth.

'We were trying to work out whether John Finley might still be stealing things somehow.' Steph frowned. 'It doesn't make sense. The Rev wants us to investigate, and when we do, he makes a fuss.'

'It is odd, I agree,' said the inspector.

'So who is this Rev?' asked Tasha.

'He's the reason we're investigating,' said Steph. 'He's a recent ghost. He was a member of the Athenaeum, and he's causing trouble. He says the ghost of an evil man is roaming on the ground floor. We've identified the guy, a petty thief called John Finley, but he's a minor criminal, as far as we know, who won't come when he's summoned.'

'Right,' said Tasha. 'So he hasn't stolen anything from this Rev.'

'Nope,' said Steph. 'I don't think they've even spoken, and the Rev didn't know his name. He just senses evil, he says. Then again, he's a bit of a snob.'

'Or there's something deeper,' said Tasha. 'I mean, I guess there could be ghosts everywhere, but why these two in particular?'

'There's a ghost librarian, too,' I said.

Tasha peered in my direction with an expression which suggested she had just missed my words. 'There's a sort of heat haze there,' she said, pointing at me.

I clapped my hands. 'She's coming on fast, isn't she?'

'I heard that,' said Tasha, looking right at me. 'I'm guessing you're Nora.'

'That's it!'

'I appreciate your joy at being seen, Nora,' said the inspector, 'but Tasha's on to something. Why is the Rev the only ghost to complain about John Finley? There could be thousands of ghosts. What's special about these two?'

'Maybe it's religious,' said Tasha. 'I mean, he's a priest and a church was there. I did a history project on Liverpool city centre at school.'

'You're full of surprises,' said Steph, and beamed at her.

'That could be it,' said Inspector Farnsworth. 'The church was there in Finley's lifetime, and churches are full of comparatively valuable things. Plate, candlesticks, even Bibles could be taken. Naturally, such a crime would affect the Rev more deeply than your average person.'

'Yes,' said Superintendent Hicks. 'And he's exactly the sort of officious busybody to make a stink about something that happened over a century ago. He always did hold a grudge.'

'This could be a way forward,' said the inspector. 'Well done, Tasha.'

'Yes, well done!' said Steph, and gave Tasha a hug. Superintendent Hicks rolled his eyes at me.

'So what happens now?' I asked.

'We mobilise,' said the inspector. 'To avoid any further incidents when the club is busy, I propose that we do it after hours. I'll phone the Athenaeum – no, I'll phone Adam first. He's essential.'

'Who's Adam?' Tasha asked. 'I feel like the new girl.'

'He's a prison warder and historian who can summon ghosts,' Steph replied.

'Of course he is,' said Tasha. 'Obvious, really.'

'Can you see me any better?' I asked.

'A bit,' said Tasha. 'I can see you're in uniform, but your face is blurry. It's like when you're at the opticians and they try different lenses. But it's definitely improving.'

'Good,' I replied. 'Can you see Superintendent Hicks?'

'He isn't as clear,' said Tasha, 'but I'm getting vibes of a grey suit and a grumpy expression.'

We all burst out laughing, except the superintendent. 'I'm not grumpy,' he said. 'I'm thinking.'

'Do let us know how that goes,' said Inspector Farnsworth. 'Right, assuming I can get everything in place, I propose that we reconvene here at nine o'clock tonight. In the meantime, I suggest you knock off a bit early to make sure you're ready for whatever happens later. Constable Saunders.'

Tasha jumped. 'Yes, sir?'

'Would you like to accompany us?'

Her face was a study. 'Umm, I think so.' She paused. 'There won't be swirly stuff, will there? Or ghosts flying around?'

'It's only our second time,' said Steph, 'but that's unlikely. It isn't *Ghostbusters* or *Harry Potter*, you know, there aren't any special effects.'

'Oh. OK.' Tasha looked a little disappointed. 'Yes, I'll come.'

'Good,' said the inspector. 'Always useful to have an extra person. Now, I believe you're needed at Erskine Street, as am I, and I suggest Constable Sharpe puts in an appearance too. Before we leave, though, you may want to, um, tidy yourselves a little.'

Steph and Tasha caught each other's eye and burst out laughing. 'Yes, sir!'

***

'Here we are yet again,' said Inspector Farnsworth, as he parked outside the Old Post Office. We weren't in a police car this time, but the inspector's own car, a bottle-green Volvo. It was quite a large car, which was as well, as there were five of us. Steph was squeezed between me and Superintendent Hicks in the back.

I had asked her privately whether she would mind sitting in the middle as, to be honest, the superintendent was driving me round the bend. Once our living colleagues had left that afternoon, he muttered that he was going to the detective offices and did not wish to be disturbed. I may have popped in once or twice, to see how he was and whether he needed anything – and yes, because I was bored – but he just told me to get out. It was like being alive all over again.

'What are you doing?' I asked.

'Told you. Thinking. And I do that better when I'm not being chattered to.'

'Suit yourself,' I said, and flounced out.

Even when the others arrived, he had said little beyond good evening.

'Something on your mind, Superintendent?' said Inspector Farnsworth.

'Yes, if you must know,' Superintendent Hicks replied. 'There's a missing piece in the puzzle, and I'm trying to work out what it is.'

The inspector smiled. 'Hopefully we can solve it tonight.'

The superintendent had been silent in the car too, and he had positively scowled when Steph said 'Here's Adam's car.' I hoped he wasn't planning to complicate things by revealing his suspicions about Adam. However, we reached the Athenaeum without any confrontations, and I hoped that once we were inside, Superintendent Hicks would be focused on the business at hand.

'I'm terribly sorry for making you do overtime,' said Inspector Farnsworth, as soon as Jude opened the door. 'And for the disturbance earlier. But I sincerely hope that this time we can resolve things once and for all.'

'I hope so too,' said Jude. He was a little less well groomed than usual: his tie had gone and his top button was undone. Given the time, I couldn't blame him. 'Do you need me to come with you? Or should I take any precautions?'

'It's probably best you aren't in attendance,' said Adam. 'There may be some disturbing scenes.'

'Right,' said Jude, looking suspicious. 'I'll ask you to sign in. Just in case we need names for any purpose.' I couldn't tell from his expression whether he thought he might be calling for police backup or contacting our next of kin.

Our four visible colleagues signed in and we proceeded to the cloakroom we had visited earlier that day. 'Wow,' said Tasha. 'Even the cloakroom's posh.'

'It is,' said Adam. 'Now, I suggest you stand back while I attempt the summons.'

We all shuffled backwards. Adam took a small

square of yellow paper from his trouser pocket, consulted it, and raised his right hand.

Tasha's nose wrinkled. 'What's that smell?' she exclaimed.

I sniffed, and caught a whiff of sickly sweet cologne. 'The Rev's here.' I turned, and saw him standing in the doorway.

'Who goes there?' he said, and chortled. 'I heard you enter and came to see what was going on.'

'Indeed, Reverend Bell,' said Inspector Farnsworth. 'Hopefully your rest will be disturbed no longer. We are about to summon John Finley.'

'We are,' said Adam, his white eyebrows drawing together slightly. 'I must request silence from everybody.'

'As the grave,' said the Rev, and chuckled again.

Adam faced away from us and raised his hand a little higher. 'John Finley, you are wanted for questioning on the matter of stealing church property. Show yourself!'

We waited. I stared around the cloakroom, my heart in my mouth. Time stretched to a thin thread. *Surely this time…*

As I was about to give up hope, the air in front of Adam shimmered. He stepped back, arm still raised, and gradually the shimmer became a mist, then a fog, and darkened to dirty brown. Clearer and clearer it grew, until it resolved itself into the shape of a short stocky man holding up his hands. His shirt was streaked with dirt and blood. He was unshaven, and dark curly hair with threads of grey hung in his eyes. His jaw appeared swollen, and his face was dark with bruises.

'That's him!' shouted the Rev. 'That's the man! Bring him to justice!'

The man swallowed. His deep-set eyes took us all in, and he croaked something.

Inspector Farnsworth stepped forward. 'Good evening. Are you John Finley?'

After a pause, the man nodded.

'I'm afraid I didn't catch what you said. Could you repeat it for me, please?'

The man swallowed again. 'Y–you got me.'

CHAPTER 16

'We . . . got you?' said Inspector Farnsworth.

'Yus. I ain't gonna deny it.' I leaned forward to hear John Finley better. As the Rev had said, his accent was strong and he was missing some teeth, but what made him harder to understand was that he muttered, as if ashamed of what he was saying. 'I regretted it near the minute I did it, but then it was too late.'

Superintendent Hicks and I looked at each other. Could it really be this easy?

'What did you do?' asked the inspector. 'We know about the food you stole. Was there something else?'

John Finley hung his head and stared at his worn-out boots. 'Are you the police?'

'We are,' said Inspector Farnsworth. 'And I should warn you that while we can't arrest or charge you, there may be a power that can.'

'Can't be worse than this.' John Finley glanced

around him, then returned to contemplating his boots. 'Every day in here, among fine things I could never afford – not that I need them now – and knowing I can never undo what I did.'

Steph moved forward until she was standing next to the inspector. 'It might help you to tell us. To get it out of your system. As Inspector Farnsworth said, we can't arrest you.'

'Maybe,' said John Finley. 'It's hard, talking to people after so long. When I came here first, when the church was still standing, I used to hide in the back pew when the service was on, worried someone would spot me. Then I worked out I was invisible. People looked through me, ignored me, sometimes sat where I was. But they didn't see me much in life, either. People only saw me when I got caught doing something wrong.'

'I'm sorry,' said Steph.

He glanced up. 'How did you catch me?'

I decided to jump in before any of my living colleagues mentioned the internet. 'We checked the records,' I said. 'That's how we found out who you were. Prison records, and others.'

He studied me. 'You're like me. How come I've never seen you here?'

'I can travel,' I replied. 'I'm a police officer, so I go where work takes me.'

'That sounds interesting,' said John Finley. 'Didn't

know women could do that.'

'Never mind all this chitchat!' the Rev shouted from behind us. 'Find out what he did! Don't let him soft-soap you with hard-luck stories. I know his type.'

'Reverend Bell, will you kindly be quiet!' snapped Inspector Farnsworth. It was the angriest I had ever seen him. 'I'm sorry, Mr Finley. If you wouldn't mind continuing…'

'Mr Finley.' He chuckled. 'That's new. You probably won't call me that when I finish talking.' He paused, thinking. 'It started with the collection plate.'

'He stole the plate! A thief in the house of God!'

Inspector Farnsworth swung round and glared at the Rev.

'I didn't steal the plate, you silly old man. How would I do that without someone seeing? No, I stole *from* the plate. I'd get hold of a silver sixpence – might be a real one, might not – and make a palaver of putting it in the plate. Then I'd say, "Oh, I need thruppence back." I'd take two pennies, then pinch a sixpence or a shilling before passing the plate on. I did it most Sundays.'

'Disgraceful,' muttered the Rev, shaking his head.

'Well, yes and no. The priest said the collection was for the needy of the parish, and I was one of the needy. Me, and my family. If helping myself to a little bit from the collection kept us out of the workhouse, it was worth it. I don't know where the collection went once they'd taken it up, but I never knew anyone who saw a penny of it. I wish I'd stopped there.'

'What else did you do, Mr Finley?' Steph asked.

'I used to think I'd regret it till the day I died,' said John Finley. 'I didn't know it would go further than that. I won't try to defend myself. What I did was wrong. I knew even as I did it. But our boots were in holes and we were half starved. I wasn't in my right mind. All that shiny silver gleaming, and someone had left a little candlestick on the corner of the pew. I waited until everyone knelt to pray and slipped it in my pocket. But when I took it to a pawnbroker the next day – not my usual one, I couldn't have looked him in the eye – he said it was pewter and gave me a shilling.'

He studied his boots again. 'I wanted to get the money somehow to buy it back and put it where it should be, but how? Stealing from the plate would've made it worse. Whatever I earned, I never had a shilling to spare, not once the family were fed and more or less clothed. In the end, I took us to London to get away from it and make a fresh start.' He gazed at the snake tattoo on his right hand. 'But I couldn't. It was still there, in my dreams.'

'AHEM.'

We jumped and looked round, although of course there was nothing to see. The voice was different from the last time I had heard it, in HMP Liverpool. Was that because it echoed less here, or—

'Here it comes,' murmured John Finley, gazing upwards. 'I don't know what it is, but I reckon this is it.'

'JOHN FINLEY, YOU HAVE MADE A FULL CONFESSION OF THE CRIMES THAT WERE OUTSTANDING. YOU ACTED IN THE INTEREST OF YOUR FAMILY.'

John Finley shifted from foot to foot. 'Yes, but—'

'THE REAL CRIME RELATES TO THE CHURCH WHICH FAILED TO HELP YOU IN YOUR HOUR OF NEED, AND THE PAWNBROKER WHO SWINDLED YOU. THE CANDLESTICK WAS MADE OF SILVER.'

'I flaming knew it!' he muttered.

'IN YOUR TIME HERE, JOHN FINLEY, YOU HAVE MORE THAN SERVED YOUR SENTENCE. CASE DISMISSED.'

'What?' cried the Rev. 'You can't do that!'

'I JUST DID.'

'Here, what's this?' John Finley was staring at his hand, which had almost disappeared. 'I feel funny. Like pins and needles, everywhere.'

'John, I think you're going to your rest,' I said.

'Will I see Susie? And the kids – all the kiddies?' His voice grew fainter as he traced the tattooed stars on his hand. 'Will there be harps and clouds, like they said in Sunday school?' Then he was gone.

I let out my breath.

'IS THAT ALL?' the voice boomed. *'IF IT IS—'*

'There may be something else.'

We all stared at Superintendent Hicks, who had taken a step forward.

'What?' said the Rev, peevishly. 'I've got rid of that nasty little man, and now I can enjoy the rest of my existence.'

'About that,' said Superintendent Hicks. 'There's been something funny about this case and I've struggled to put my finger on it. But I think I've worked it out.'

'Go on, then,' said the Rev. 'Spit it out, man.'

'I intend to,' said the superintendent. 'Tell me this, Reverend Bell. How could a man like you, a priest in a poor parish, possibly afford to be a member of the Athenaeum in the nineteen-sixties?'

The Rev drew himself up. 'I spent the savings acquired by frugal living on improving my mind and joining a community of worthy individuals.'

'Frugal living,' said Superintendent Hicks. 'I remember when you used to come to the Bridewell, complaining of noise and horseplay. When you were railing on the subject of guttersnipes who should be taught a lesson, I remember thinking that your boots were better than mine – and I was a superintendent on a good wage. Your suits were pretty sharp, too, and that cologne you wore, revolting as it is, didn't come for free.'

'How dare you question my integrity?' thundered the Rev. 'How dare you insult a man of the cloth?'

'I dare because I remember those charity appeals you ran,' said Superintendent Hicks. 'You called on the great and the good and put adverts in the paper, requesting donations for a day out for the poor.'

'They got a day out! It was all above board. Fair and square.'

'One of my men helped out at one of your days, Reverend,' said Superintendent Hicks. 'A picnic in Grant Gardens, probably ten minutes' walk from your church. Sandwiches and lemonade, and an apple for afters. I wonder where the rest of the money went.'

'Then you'll have to wonder,' the Rev retorted. 'As if any accounts still exist, sixty years on.'

Superintendent Hicks walked over to him. 'Reverend Bell, I don't doubt that you have destroyed anything which would prove your appropriation of charitable funds, but that doesn't prove your innocence.'

A slow smile spread over the Rev's face. 'You can prove nothing.'

'THAT'S WHAT YOU THINK.'

We all jumped again.

'REVEREND NORMAN BELL, WE CANNOT DECLARE YOUR GUILT OR INNOCENCE. YOU MAY HAVE DESTROYED RECORDS

DELIBERATELY. YOU MAY HAVE ASSUMED THAT NO ONE IS STILL ALIVE WHO CAN TESTIFY AGAINST YOU—'

'Exactly,' said the Rev. 'And that doesn't mean I'm admitting anything.'

'YOU DO NOT HAVE TO. IN MY WORLD, A WITNESS DOES NOT HAVE TO BE ALIVE TO TESTIFY AGAINST YOU. I HAVE ALL THE TIME IN THE WORLD TO FIND WITNESSES.'

The Rev swallowed. 'Stop it,' he muttered. He coughed, and fumbled with the top button of his shirt.

'*COME WITH ME.*' And the Rev was switched off like a light.

***

'Well done, Superintendent,' said Inspector Farnsworth. 'I had no idea.'

'It was less an idea than a suspicion,' said Superintendent Hicks. 'I knew in my heart that he was a wrong 'un. I should have listened to myself earlier.' But he wasn't looking at us as he spoke. He was staring at his hand.

'Are you all right?' I asked.

He met my eyes. 'Yes. I thought that maybe…'

'That you might go to your rest?' I smiled. 'I reckon you've got a bit more investigating to do first.'

Tasha went to one of the benches by the wall and sat down heavily. 'Is it always like this?'

'I don't know about always,' said Inspector

Farnsworth. 'But that seems fairly typical, yes.'

'Good grief.' Tasha pushed her hair off her face and slumped on the bench, staring into space. Steph sat beside her and put an arm round her shoulders.

Inspector Farnsworth surveyed us. 'The case is out of our hands now. I'll go and tell Jude that the ghosts have gone and everything should be back to normal.' He put his hands in his pockets and strolled out of the cloakroom.

I looked around the room. Steph and Tasha were leaning against each other, exhausted. The ghost of Superintendent Hicks was staring at his hand. Adam, a being who wasn't a ghost but didn't seem entirely human either, was examining a plaster moulding. And then there was me, a matron who had somehow achieved the promotion of her dreams a hundred years after she joined the force. What a crew we were. 'Normal, indeed.' I grinned. 'I'll believe that when I see it.'

CHAPTER 17

Tasha dropped the last file on the teetering pile. 'That's another drawer emptied.'

'Yep,' said Steph. 'Let's get them in the box.'

Tasha lifted a plastic crate onto the file-room table. 'Oof!' she exclaimed. 'That's getting heavy.'

Steph lifted the pile and put it in the crate. 'It'll be worse now. But at least they're dealt with, and no one will have to look at them again.'

I have to say that getting Tasha on board had been a godsend. It had taken less than fifteen minutes of Steph moaning about the files for her to say 'Then why don't you get rid of the ones that don't matter? I'm sure there's a record disposal contract with someone. No one will be interested in these, not after all this time. In fact, it's probably our duty to shred them. Data protection, and that.' She had taken over the laptop for a few minutes, then pointed in triumph to a table on the screen. 'There. We have to get rid of them.'

And so, one day, a van pulled up outside and a man brought in a stack of blue plastic crates. 'Call us when you want them picking up, duck,' he said, and drove away.

Steph looked at the clock on the wall. 'Well, it's quarter past five, and I don't fancy starting another crate.'

'I don't think there is another crate,' said Tasha. 'So we're free!' She spun round in a slow circle, arms waving.

'We should book the pick-up for tomorrow morning,' said Steph. '*Then* we're free.'

Tasha pushed her hair back, then regarded her fingers critically. 'Is that a cobweb?'

'Let me see,' said Steph. 'Euww!'

'You're no better,' said Tasha. 'We both need a shower.'

'What a good idea,' said Steph, grinning.

'We're still here, you know,' said Superintendent Hicks. 'Why don't you two lock the file room and have a cup of tea upstairs.'

Tasha giggled. 'Is that because you're going to talk about us, Superintendent?'

'No,' said Superintendent Hicks, with dignity. 'It's because all this canoodling is enough to make anyone sick.'

'Right you are, sir,' said Steph. Tasha saluted the

superintendent, and after saying goodbye, they went upstairs.

Once their laughter had faded, we went upstairs too and drifted into the yard. Prince and Queen Vic were in the corner, but ventured out to meet us.

'Young love, eh,' said the superintendent.

'I assume you mean Steph and Tasha.'

He snorted. 'These two are a bit past it. Aren't you, old boy?' Prince whickered and stuck his nose into the superintendent's hand, probably out of habit.

'I think it's nice. And Steph's much happier. Let them have their fun, I say.'

Superintendent Hicks shot me a look from under his eyebrows. 'Do you wish you'd had your fun, Nora?'

'Who's to say I didn't?' I walked to Queen Vic and stroked her flank.

'Oh, um, I didn't mean— That is, with you being a Miss, I naturally assumed…'

I couldn't help laughing. 'I walked out with a boy or two, Superintendent. While I can't have that sort of fun now, there's still fun to be had. Investigating fun. And it will be more fun with Tasha on board. She's a good addition to the team.'

The team. I was finally part of a team, not just an insignificant matron struggling to be heard. I continued to stroke Queen Vic, lost in thought.

'You'll wear a hole in that horse if you carry on,'

said Superintendent Hicks, bringing out his pipe.

'Oh. Sorry,' I said to Queen Vic, who flicked her ears at me. I tried to think of something to say. 'Oh yes, I know what I wanted to ask you. What were you talking to Adam about?'

'Adam?' The superintendent knocked his pipe against the wall, not that anything came out.

'Yes, that evening after – you know. You asked if you could have a word. I'd forgotten; there's been so much to do.'

Superintendent Hicks pulled out his tobacco pouch and began to fill his pipe. 'I told him I recognised the age spot on his hand, and asked him who or what he was.'

A chill ran through me. 'And?'

He pushed down the tobacco with his thumb. 'Sure you want to know?'

I swallowed, a reaction left over from being alive. 'I think so. Unless… Will it change my opinion of him?'

He smiled. 'I doubt it. He told me there was no great mystery. He was one of the original warders when the jail opened, in 1855.'

'So you were right!' I cried.

'Of course. He was a junior then, but he came to the notice of the head warden, who put him in charge of the prison records. There he stayed. But when he was nearing retirement age, Adam realised he wasn't ageing any more than he already had. He didn't grow weaker and his mind stayed sharp. At the same time, he was less inclined to go to places that didn't involve the prison or its history in any way. Like us and the Bridewell, he had somehow become bound to the prison and the lives of its inmates, past and present. And there he is today, however many years on.'

I studied Superintendent Hicks to see if he was having a little joke with me, but he seemed completely sincere. 'Do you believe him?'

The superintendent considered, then shrugged. 'There's no reason not to. I mean, I didn't believe in ghosts until I saw one.'

'Who was your first ghost?'

He rummaged in his pocket for matches and turned away to light his pipe. He didn't speak again till he had got it going. Then he looked at me. 'You were.'

'Me?' I had never thought about it from the superintendent's point of view. 'When was that?'

'Not long after word came to the station that you had died from the Spanish flu. I went to the front desk and there you were, reading over the sergeant's shoulder. I nearly fainted. I went out for a pipe sharpish, and pondered what to do. Since no one else could see you, I decided it was best to pretend you weren't there. I'd probably have lost my job if I'd let on.'

'Oh.' That was all I could say. I understood why

Superintendent Hicks had done it, but how I wished he hadn't.

'I'm so sorry.' He did seem truly woebegone. 'If I could turn the clock back, knowing what I know now… But I had a wife, and a family, and – I was scared.' He looked lost in a way that I had never seen before.

'It's all right.' I suspected he wanted me to say that I forgave him, but I wasn't quite ready for that. 'Water under the bridge. And we can still be friends.'

'Can we?' His eyes were shining.

'Course we can. Anyway, get yourself together, Superintendent. The inspector will be here any minute.'

'Indeed he will.'

The Chief had been extremely pleased with our restoration of peace at the Athenaeum. He had even come to the Bridewell, at the inspector's invitation. 'Good work, everyone,' he boomed. 'I was a bit worried at times, but in the end you came through. Well done.' He reached into his inner jacket pocket and gave Inspector Farnsworth an envelope.

'What's this, sir?' the inspector asked.

'You'd better open it and see, hadn't you?'

The inspector ripped it open. 'Oh!' he exclaimed.

'I thought a membership to the Athenaeum was the least I could do. Had a word with a couple of people. You'll like it, Farnsworth. Lots of your sort there:

quiet, bookish types. And there's a couple of guest passes, if you want to take the wife. Or the constables here, perhaps.'

'Thank you, Chief Inspector, that's most kind.'

'Think nothing of it,' said the Chief. 'Anyway. Got to be at a memorial lunch in half an hour. Carry on.' And off he went.

'Don't feel you have to take Tasha and me to the Athenaeum, Inspector,' Steph had said, immediately. 'I'm not sure it's our sort of thing.'

'Don't worry, Steph,' Inspector Farnsworth had replied, with a smile. 'I have a better idea.'

***

'I hear a car,' said Superintendent Hicks, pointing his nose towards the street.

I listened. 'So do I. I think that's him.' Sure enough, the inspector's Volvo drew up outside the gates not long after.

Inspector Farnsworth opened his window. 'Come on, then,' he said, and we hurried to meet him.

The Athenaeum was busier than one might have thought in the evening. I suppose lots of people came when they had finished work. I exclaimed at the huge Christmas tree in the entrance hall, groaning with lights and decorations, but the superintendent took it in his stride.

'Library?' asked Inspector Farnsworth.

'Please,' we said together.

As the current librarian welcomed the inspector, we saw Mr Chapman hurrying over. 'Do you have passes?' he demanded.

'You know we have passes, Mr Chapman,' said Superintendent Hicks. 'We're with the inspector, and he always carries two guest passes.'

The librarian drifted across and peered at the papers the inspector was holding, then returned. 'Very well. What do you wish to look at today?'

'What would you recommend?' asked Superintendent Hicks.

'We have an extensive record of the books and magazines that have been damaged over the years, and therefore destroyed. Would you like to see it?'

'We'd love to,' I replied.

Mr Chapman, clearly delighted to have something to do, fetched a large, leather-bound volume and set it on an empty table. 'We have several early issues of the *Liverpool Daily Post*, a good selection of the *Illustrated London News*, some of the works of Baroness Orczy…'

'Have you got *The Scarlet Pimpernel*?' I asked.

He ran his finger down a column. 'We have.'

'Oh my! Yes, please!'

'And for sir?'

The superintendent peered at the book. 'I'll take *Ivanhoe*, if you don't mind. Read it as a boy. Always meant to pick it up again, and never did.'

'Right away, sir, madam.' Mr Chapman bustled off and returned with two smallish transparent books. 'I've taken the liberty of bringing the first volumes. When you're ready for the second, let me know. Of course, these cannot leave the library.'

'Understood,' said the superintendent.

We took our books and settled at a quiet table in the corner. Presently Inspector Farnsworth joined us, carrying a bound volume of his own. '*Police Gazette*, 1884,' he murmured. 'I wonder if I'll find John Finley in here.'

'At least we found him in real life,' I said. 'And we brought the Rev to justice.'

'We did,' said the inspector, quietly. 'Not that we can ever tell the Athenaeum about it. But we've done our job, and now we can rest.'

'Till the next time,' rumbled Superintendent Hicks.

I grinned. 'You make it sound like a toast, Superintendent. Till the next time!'

Superintendent Hicks actually smiled, then lifted *Ivanhoe* and held it up as if proposing a toast. Inspector Farnsworth raised his eyebrows, then did the same with his book. I grabbed *The Scarlet Pimpernel* and followed suit. 'Till the next time,' we chorused, then leaned forward and carefully, so as not to annoy Mr Chapman, touched our books together.

WHAT TO READ NEXT

Nora and Steph (and their various colleagues) return in The Spirit of the Law book 3, *The Case of the Lost Treasure.*

When Tasha agrees to help her ghost colleague Nora solve a cold case, everything changes.

Tasha was in her sergeant's good books. Now she's in disgrace and her in-tray's full of paperwork. Worst of all, her partner Steph is growing suspicious.

The case is far from straightforward. Mary, a young woman from the Regency period, is haunting St John's Gardens in search of her child. However, she is troubled by the ghost hunters chasing strange noises in nearby St George's Hall. Is there another ghost? If so, why is it making its presence known?

ACKNOWLEDGEMENTS

As ever, my first thanks go to my superb beta readers – Carol Bissett, Ruth Cunliffe, Paula Harmon, and Stephen Lenhardt – and my very speedy proofreader, John Croall. Thank you so much for all your help! Any errors that remain are mine only.

If you've read the first book in the series, *The Case of the Four Fingers*, you may recall that it came about through a tour of the Bridewell Studios and Gallery on a Heritage Open Day (https://www.bridewellstudiosliverpool.org). Funnily enough, when an idea for book two started to formulate in my mind, it came from another visit I made on the same day, to the Athenaeum in Liverpool (yes, it is real!). I'd like to thank the Athenaeum for opening their doors on Heritage Open Day last year, for allowing me to use the club in a book, and for answering my questions. While I've tried to describe the building accurately, I should stress that as far as I know it doesn't have any ghosts! I also added a sneaky fictional cloakroom for summoning purposes… You can find out more about the Athenaeum here: https://theathenaeum.org.uk/.

The Digital Panopticon is also real (though John Finley isn't) and can be found here: https://www.digitalpanopticon.org/. I consulted several maps of Liverpool, and there's a great list here: https://liverpool1207blog.wordpress.com/old-liverpool-maps/.

Finally, many thanks to you, the reader. I hope you've enjoyed this book, and if you have, please consider leaving a short review or a rating on Amazon and/or Goodreads. Reviews and ratings are immensely important to authors, as they help books find new readers.

COVER CREDITS

Image (rotated, edited and coloured): 'staircase' by avidd: https://flickr.com/photos/avidd/1876101604/. Public domain.

Cover font: IM FELL Great Primer Pro by Igino Marini: https://www.fontsquirrel.com/fonts/im-fell-great-primer-pro. License: SIL Open Font License v1.10: https://www.fontsquirrel.com/license/im-fell-great-primer-pro.

ABOUT THE AUTHOR

Liz Hedgecock grew up in London, England, did an English degree, and then took forever to start writing. After several years working in the National Health Service, some short stories crept into the world. A few even won prizes. Then the stories started to grow longer…

Now Liz travels between the nineteenth and twenty-first centuries, murdering people. To be fair, she does usually clean up after herself.

Liz's reimaginings of Sherlock Holmes, the Magical Bookshop series, her Pippa Parker cozy mystery series, the Booker & Fitch and Caster & Fleet mystery series (with Paula Harmon), and the Maisie Frobisher Mysteries are available in ebook and paperback.

Liz lives in Cheshire with her husband and two sons, and when she's not writing or child-wrangling you can usually find her reading, messing about on Twitter, or cooing over stuff in museums and art galleries. That's her story, anyway, and she's sticking to it.

Website/blog: http://lizhedgecock.wordpress.com
Facebook: http://www.facebook.com/lizhedgecockwrites
Twitter: http://twitter.com/lizhedgecock
Goodreads: https://www.goodreads.com/lizhedgecock

BOOKS BY LIZ HEDGECOCK

To check out my books, please visit my Amazon author page: http://author.to/LizH (global link). If you follow me there, you'll be notified when I release a new book.

The Magical Bookshop (6 novels)
An eccentric owner, a hostile cat, and a bookshop with a mind of its own. Can Jemma turn around the second-worst secondhand bookshop in London? And can she learn its secrets?

Pippa Parker Mysteries (6 novels)
Meet Pippa Parker: mum, amateur sleuth, and resident of a quaint English village called Much Gadding. And then the murders began…

Booker & Fitch Mysteries (5 novels, with Paula Harmon)
Jade Fitch hopes for a fresh start when she opens a new-age shop in a picturesque market town. Meanwhile, Fi Booker runs a floating bookshop as well as dealing with her teenage son. And as soon as they meet, it's murder…

Caster & Fleet Mysteries (6 novels, with Paula Harmon)

There's a new detective duo in Victorian London – and they're women! Meet Katherine and Connie, two young women who become partners in crime. Solving it, that is!

Mrs Hudson & Sherlock Holmes (3 novels)
Mrs Hudson is Sherlock Holmes's elderly landlady. Or is she? Find out her real story here.

Maisie Frobisher Mysteries (4 novels)
When Maisie Frobisher, a bored young Victorian socialite, goes travelling in search of adventure, she finds more than she could ever have dreamt of. Mystery, intrigue and a touch of romance.

The Spirit of the Law (3 novellas)
Meet a detective duo – a century apart! A modern-day police constable and a hundred-year-old ghost team up to solve the coldest of cases.

Sherlock & Jack (3 novellas)
Jack has been ducking and diving all her life. But when she meets the great detective Sherlock Holmes they form an unlikely partnership. And Jack discovers that she is more important than she ever realised…

Tales of Meadley (2 novelettes)
A romantic comedy mini-series based in the village of Meadley, with a touch of mystery too.

Halloween Sherlock (3 novelettes)
Short dark tales of Sherlock Holmes and Dr Watson, perfect for a grim winter's night.

For children
A Christmas Carrot (with Zoe Harmon)
Perkins the Halloween Cat (with Lucy Shaw)
Rich Girl, Poor Girl (for 9-12 year olds)

Printed in Great Britain
by Amazon

62381297R00099